Praise for the Love and Honor Series

"Hallee writes with such authentic detail that I felt the sweat drip off my brow, heard the buzz of the African jungle, and ran for dear life with Cynthia and Rick. A rich story of courage and seeing the world with new eyes. Riveting, this book will get under your skin and into your heart. Absolutely fantastic."

Susan May Warren, *USA Today* bestselling author, on
Honor Bound

"Hallee Bridgeman weaves a military suspense with romance for a fast-paced adventure. Word of Honor kept me turning pages all night long."

DiAnn Mills, author of *Concrete Evidence*, on
Word of Honor

"What a fabulous story with perfectly crafted characters who grab your heart from the opening page. I loved everything about it—from the witty dialogue to the breath-stopping suspense to the tender romance. Once I started, I couldn't put it down. I highly recommend this book and can't wait for the next one."

Lynette Eason, award-winning, bestselling author
of the Extreme Measures series, on *Honor Bound*

"This book has something for everyone—action, adventure, romance, and true-to-life sadness and grief. Hallee crafts a complex story infused with spiritual truth, wrapped around intriguing lead characters with complicated personalities and backgrounds. Phil and Melissa will have you rooting for them the whole way through."

Janice Cantore, retired police officer and author of
Breach of Honor, on *Honor's Refuge*

LOVE IN ANY LANGUAGE

THE LOVE & HONOR SERIES

BY HALLEE BRIDGEMAN

Prequel novella

Love in Any Language

Novels by Revell

Honor Bound
Word of Honor
Honor's Refuge

Learn more online:
www.halleebridgeman.com/series/love-and-honor-series/

LOVE ★ HONOR

LOVE IN ANY LANGUAGE

HALLEE BRIDGEMAN

Olivia Kimbrell Press™

Love in Any Language,
A Love and Honor Series Prequel Novella
© 2022 by Hallee Bridgeman

Published by Olivia Kimbrell Press™
P.O. Box 470, Fort Knox, KY 40121-0470
www.oliviakimbrellpress.com

Printed in the United States of America

Library of Congress Cataloging-in-Publication Data

Names: Bridgeman, Hallee, author.

Title: Love in Any Language/ Hallee Bridgeman.

Description: Fort Knox, KY: Olivia Kimbrell Press™ [2022] | Series: Love and Honor ; 0

Identifiers: LCCN: 2022943914 | ISBN 9781681902128 (paperback) | ISBN 9781681902135 (casebound) | ISBN 9781681902081 (ebook) | ASIN: B09VDPXV1Z

Subjects: LCSH: Special forces (Military science)—Fiction. | Rescues—Fiction. | Jungle survival—Africa—Fiction. | LCGFT: Thrillers (Fiction) | Romance fiction. | Christian fiction.

LC record available at https://lccn.loc.gov/2022943914

Scripture quotations, whether quoted or paraphrased by the characters, are from THE HOLY BIBLE, NEW INTERNATIONAL VERSION®, NIV® Copyright © 1973, 1978, 1984, 2011 by Biblica, Inc.® Used by permission. All rights reserved worldwide.

Olivia Kimbrell Press™ is a publisher offering true to life, meaningful fiction from a Christian worldview intended to uplift the heart and engage the mind.

This book is dedicated to the men and women of the United States Armed Forces.
Thank you for your selfless service to our country.

Be devoted to one another in love.
Honor one another above yourselves.
—Romans 12:10

Glossary of Military Terms & Acronyms

AO: area of operations

Bird: Helicopter

CAC: Common Access Card

CHU: containerized housing unit (a small, climate-controlled shipping container)

CJSOTF-HOA: Combined Joint Special Operations Task Force-Horn of Africa

DOD: Department of Defense

exfil: exfiltrate (withdraw)

HQ: headquarters

infil: infiltrate (move in)

klick: kilometer

LOC: Logistics Operations Center

LT: Either a first or second Lieutenant.

MRE: meal ready to eat

ODA: Operational Detachment Alpha

OPCON: operational control

PCS: permanent change of station

PR: personnel recovery mission

PT: Physical training, usually organized morning exercises consisting of calisthenics and a two-mile run.

Ricky-tick: quickly and efficiently

Roger: understood and acknowledged

Roger, wilco: understood, acknowledged, and will comply

SCIF: sensitive compartmented information facility (a secure location where classified information can be reviewed)

SFODA: Special Forces Operational Detachment Alpha (an A-Team)

SIPRNET: secret internet protocol router network (a network the Department of Defense uses to transfer classified information)

SITREP: situational report

TDY: Temporary duty travel (TDY), also known as temporary additional duty (TAD), is a designation reflecting a US Armed Forces Service member's travel or other assignment at a location other than his or her permanent duty station.

Wilco: Will comply

CHAPTER

★

ONE

International Waters, Gulf of Aden

The modified Boston Whaler with sound suppressed but astonishingly powerful twin outboard engines cut through the water, slicing its way smoothly toward the fully laden third generation Suezmax container ship that loomed on the darkening horizon before them. Christened the "Bellflower" in 1987, the ship had a hauling capacity of 12,000 TEUs with a length of just under 400 meters, a breadth of 56 meters, and a draught of around 15 meters. From their perspective at sea level, the ship looked like an island.

Second Lieutenant Jorge "Pina Colada" Peña lead the team with Sergeant Daniel "Pot Pie" Swanson, Sergeant Travis "Trout" Fisher, Sergeant Gerald "Jerry Maguire" McBride, Sergeant Wade "Commando" Chandler, and Sergeant Eric "Gilligan" Gill in the boat.

The cool, salt-scented air rushed past them, and the occasional spray of salty water made droplets form on Jorge's goggles.

He glanced at the Boston Whaler to starboard loaded with Team Captain Rick Norton, aka "Daddy", Chief Warrant Officer Three Zachary "MMMBop" Hanson, Sergeant David "Mr. Miyagi" Morita, Lieutenant Philip "Doc Oz" Osbourne, and Sergeant "Honest Abe" Ibrahim. Even though he knew they were there and could almost perfectly pinpoint them, he couldn't actually see them in the dark.

Suddenly, a pair of flat gray SH-60 Seahawk helicopters swept past their small boats at an altitude of perhaps five meters off the deck. They operated without running lights, or lights of any kind, and looked effectively invisible to the naked eye. Only the propwash in the air, the ground effect on the seawater, and the noise of the General Electric T700 turboshaft engines combined with the chop of the rotors identified their presence. Within seconds the aircraft began their attack runs on the objective and their door gunners opened fire exactly on time, strafing the cargo ship's bridge, providing cover for Jorge and the five men in his team. The occasional tracer round gave him his only notion as to the positions of the aircraft in the moonless night sky.

He made out muzzle flashes from the ship. The bad guys had responded much more quickly than he would have estimated. The loud ping of a bullet ricocheting off the armored bow of his vessel made him want to duck even further behind the shields.

Closer to the ship, the noise of the small arms gunfire and rapid automatic fire from the helicopters made him glad for his earplugs. As soon as they made contact with the hull, Jorge shouted orders to tie off and climb the ladder. His radio operator, Sergeant Eric Gill, kept in contact with both Captain Norton, Headquarters, and their naval air support.

Jorge paused only a fraction of a second before grabbing the rung of the ladder and pulling himself up. This was his first mission as intel officer in this Special Forces Operations Detachment Alpha, or A-Team. This was his first combat mission since accepting his commission as a Second Lieutenant. He didn't realize how different it would feel compared to combat missions as a noncommissioned officer in a regular infantry unit. He could feel the weight of the lives of the men he led resting on his shoulders.

Training pushed the nerves down. Hand over hand, he climbed until he slid over the side of the railing and rolled smoothly on the deck with his weapon instantly in operation. He held his weapon ready, crouching and watching for enemy combatants to appear. Norton and his team boarded the ship from the other side and nearer to the bow. Before he knew it, he heard the whisper-shouted affirmation from behind him, "Last man."

Keying the microphone integrated into his gear, Jorge confirmed all aboard by subvocalizing, "Six. Four. Set." Norton offered his own confirmation in Jorge's earpiece in the form of two clicking noises. Norton's group would head down into the belly of the ship. Jorge's group would sweep the bridge and upper decks.

He gestured toward the bridge with a bladed left hand, fingers extended and joined. His right hand never wavered on his weapon. From the center of his group, he led his team across the deck toward the bridge. The two men diagonally in front of him with "Pot Pie" Swanson to his left and "Gilligan" Gill to his right kept their weapons high and low alternately. Jorge kept his weapon trained in the direction of travel. The three men behind him—"Trout" Fisher, "Jerry Maguire" McBride, and "Commando" Chandler—looked like a mirror image of Jorge and his pair as they walked backward, training their eyes in the direction of their deadly rifle muzzles.

They moved as a single unit, gliding across the deck like a six-pointed starfish with their upper bodies moving only slightly and their legs absorbing the motion involved in the swaying ship and the act of walking. To an outside observer, they would look like a twelve-legged animal whose upper body floated above a dozen skittering legs.

They reached the bridge hatch without incident and the men pulling rear guard stacked, "Trout" Fisher and "Jerry Maguire" McBride dropping to a one-kneed crouch while "Commando" Chandler remained standing. All of them swept the surrounding area prepared to fire. "Pot Pie" Swanson tried the bridge door and found it locked. He made a dismissive gesture with one hand before returning his grip to his weapon.

Jorge tapped Swanson on the shoulder and gestured with his left hand making a cutting motion, then stepped back with his spine against the bulkhead beside the hatch.

As Swanson affixed a tetrahedron shaped pinch of composition four, or C-4, along with a foot of detonation cord on the hatch handle, they all moved to the side for cover from the blast. "Fire in the hole in three," Swanson quietly announced into his mic. After a slow count to three-Mississippi, Swanson detonated the charge.

Jorge went high and Gill went in low as they swung through the now open doorway, weapons ready. A man in red and white ghutrah and a black vest with bandoliers crisscrossed over his chest raised a Kalashnikov AK-74 toward Jorge, who fired two shots, dropping the man before he could even fire a single shot. The other man on the bridge, wearing a brown ghutrah with his blue suit jacket held both of his hands up and stepped away from his fallen comrade. While Jorge kept his gun trained on him, Chandler moved forward, quickly searching him before zip-tying his hands behind his back.

A few days from now, assuming he lived through this

mission, Jorge would cope with the fact that he had just taken a man's life. He would let the remorse of that act wash over him and through him and he would pray and get right with the God who he knew without a shred of doubt created him to be a soldier. Right now, he had no time to deal with any of those emotions. Right now, he had a job to do and lives depended upon him doing it well.

Jorge walked over to the zip tied man who crouched on his knees on the deck. He placed the muzzle of his M-4 carbine below the man's chin so he could smell the fresh cordite and feel the warmth of the steel from the recently fired rounds. Then he used the muzzle to raise the man's face until their eyes met. He would never fire on a prisoner, but he needed his prisoner to believe, without a single doubt, that he would. So he began his street-theater performance. The look he gave the prisoner informed him that he would not hesitate to take this man's life as well. "Speak English?"

The man carefully shook his head and said, "La. 'Ana 'atahadath alearabia." No. I speak Arabic.

Jorge nodded, maintaining eye contact. He slowly, deliberately, and very calmly slid his finger onto the trigger of his weapon watching the man's fear increase as he did so. In accented Arabic, he demanded, "How many with you?"

When his prisoner didn't answer instantly, he gave the man's chin a little tap with the muzzle of his M-4 carbine and cut his eyes toward the corpse leaking blood onto the deck just a few feet away. "We can just find them and ask them."

"Khamsa. Khamsa." The man pleaded. Five.

Jorge instantly removed his finger from the trigger and lowered his weapon. To Gill, he nodded and said, "That tracks."

Gill gave an affirmation in the radio and said, "Norton's taking fire near the living quarters below decks."

Jorge nodded. "Right. We're good here. Pot Pie, Trout, Jerry Maguire, go lend the boss a hand. Gill, send RSVPs on their behalf." Gill quietly informed Captain Norton that three friendlies were en route in support.

While they searched the bridge for information, he could hear the chatter of the team as they killed one more bad guy and, after chasing him through ductwork in between the decks, found Haafiz Durrani, one their mission targets. As the intelligence officer, Jorge knew Durrani was a senior lieutenant for the terrorist Kamyar Punjabi, their primary mission target.

Gill glanced at Jorge. "No Punjabi?"

"Maybe he's hiding in with the crew. He's slick like a bucket of eels."

Over the radio, they heard his three-man detachment calling out, "Friendlies. Friendlies. Friendlies."

Jorge listened intently as his men integrated with Norton's team and they all began to lay down disciplined—and deadly accurate—suppressive fire. The firefight didn't last much longer. The pirates surrendered quickly with two dead and one wounded.

★ ★ ★

Jorge took Hanson's report while leaning against the bulkhead near the locked hatch of the cabin that contained Durrani. "They shoved the crew into a single stateroom—all twenty-four of them." Fury dripped from Hanson's voice. "We counted eighteen able seamen, two cooks, three engineers, and one dead captain."

With a nod, Jorge said, "Thanks, Chief. Ozzy get a look at them?"

"Yeah. A few minor injuries. Dehydrated, hungry. Exhausted. He's getting them fed some soup. No Punjabi."

Norton came down the passageway from the direction of sick bay, and pointed at the other end of the P-way. "She's here."

Jorge lifted an eyebrow. "She?"

"Selah."

Thinking of the stone-faced terrorist on the other side of the door, he wondered what information a woman codenamed Selah could effectively extract. "Sir...."

Norton cut him off, and his beard lifted as he smiled. "You gotta have faith, Pina Colada. Trust your daddy. Father knows best."

Nothing in Jorge's entire life led him to trust any other person so blindly—except in the case of Captain Rick Norton, the leader of this A-Team. He actually carried the lives of all eleven men in his hands, and he gave the same kind of trust he expected in return.

Norton walked down the hall and looked up the

staircase. "Well, don't you look a sight, twenty-four-ten."

"Daddy," came the reply. He detected a very faint Texas twang in the husky alto voice. "Been too long."

Jorge watched her walk in his direction. She didn't bother to duck her head as she entered through the hatch. She couldn't be taller than five-two with a thin build to match. She wore a pair of black cargo pants and a black long-sleeved button-down linen shirt. In her hand, she held a black scarf.

"Selah, this is Lieutenant Jorge Peña, our new intel officer. Peña, meet Sergeant Emma Selah. She's the best tactical debriefer I've ever seen. I requested her due to our somewhat urgent need for timely and accurate information."

Jorge couldn't believe the United States Army's Special Forces would rely on this tiny woman with her husky voice and deep, dark brown eyes to do anything at all. He raised an eyebrow. "Looking forward to watching you work," he said.

She stuck the edge of the scarf in her pocket and produced a hair band. While she clutched it between her teeth, she gathered her long black hair behind her head, then secured it with the band. She maintained eye contact with him while she worked to change her appearance.

"I think I detect a whisker of doubt in your expression, Lieutenant." She wrapped the scarf around her head then secured the end over the bottom half of her face. Suddenly, she looked like a Persian princess. To complete the look, she pulled a compact mirror and black eye pencil out of a cargo pocket and expertly applied dark liner to her eyes. She made a circling motion around her face. "Facial recognition," she explained. "Y'all have beards. I have to make do."

It actually made sense to him. He just wondered how or why a man from a culture with so little respect for women would willingly answer questions proposed by a woman dressed like that.

She gestured at the door. "Understand you had no luck getting him to talk. Has that changed since I left shore?"

Jorge shook his head. "He's not budging."

She put her hand on the hatch handle and said to Norton, "What's the timetable?"

"Intel put it at dawn."

Jorge's stomach twisted almost painfully. A nuclear bomb targeting the densely populated Gaza Strip would detonate in six short hours if they couldn't locate it.

She looked up at Jorge and said, "I'd like you to join me, LT. But, keep your mouth shut. Don't mess with my system. You're just there to analyze information." She sized him up. He could almost see her thoughts on her face as she analyzed his swarthy appearance and processed his ethnic sounding given and surnames. "*Claro?*"

He glanced at Norton. His new captain grinned in a way he'd never seen before. Not knowing what to make of that, he looked back at her and answered, "English is fine. And yes. Crystal clear."

She opened the hatch and walked in, her size four feet barely making any noise on the metal deck plates. Haafiz

Durrani's eyes widened in surprise as much as Jorge had felt. When he met her eyes, she spoke in perfect unaccented Arabic. "*Sabah El Kheir*." Good morning.

He scoffed and leaned back, unconsciously trying to create distance between himself and Emma Selah.

Without waiting for permission, Emma smoothly sat in the chair across from him, closing the space between them, making a show of smoothing her slacks and her scarf before continuing. This time when she greeted him, she chose a greeting more familiar to the regions of Lebanon and Syria. "*Sah El Nom*, Alsayyid Durrani." Good morning, Mister Durrani.

When his eyes widened, she continued still in Arabic but now with a strongly Syrian inflection. "We need to know where the device is. Bonus points for giving us Kamyar Punjabi." She paused. "You have exactly twenty minutes to give me this information."

CHAPTER

TWO

The bright Texas sun shone through the car windows. Emma pulled the sun visor down as she maneuvered through her parents' neighborhood. When she got to their cul-de-sac, she pulled into the driveway and killed the engine. Instead of getting out, she stared at the little brick house nestled in a suburb of San Antonio.

On the heels of nine-eleven, her father had helped American soldiers gain a foothold against the Taliban. He'd done that at great risk to his life and his family's life, but he'd done it with the full blessing of her mom. In the end, the Taliban put a price on his head. In the summer of 2002, her family had to flee Afghanistan.

To thank him for his assistance, America offered them sanctuary. Her father got a job as a Department of Defense civilian teaching soldiers about the enemy's way of life, beliefs, and languages. A local church adopted them, helped them get a house, and gave her mother a job at the church's daycare. Emma spoke English well enough to teach her brother and by the time school began, he spoke well enough to enter kindergarten.

Emma had spent many hours around her parents' table with their new friends from the church. The mutual respect between her father and the pastor generated hours of healthy discourse. Eventually, her father became a follower of Christ. Her mother had become a believer a few months before him. Soon their entire family worshipped together in the big church on the corner of their street.

An unconscious grin adorned her face at the relief of parking in her parent's driveway. She tapped her horn and opened the car door. The front door to the brick house opened, and Emma's mom, Zara, rushed out. Emma barely had a chance to get out of the car before her mom's arms came around her. "Oh, my dear," her mom exclaimed. "I have been watching for you for hours."

Emma had graduated high school taking dual credits at the local community college. She had enlisted in the National Guard to get the Montgomery GI Bill so that she could pay her way through college without adding a financial burden to her parents. At twenty, she graduated from Texas A & M with a dual degree in linguistics and political science. She considered accepting a commission but instead had enlisted in the active Army to fulfill her military obligation. Between her language skills and training, she'd looked forward to a very successful career.

But the constant deployments had exhausted her. When the corporate headhunter representing a government contractor approached her about utilizing her skills as a contractor for the military, she originally bucked. Why should she quit serving the country she loved? But when the benefits packet came in, it swayed her. She could go on an assignment and come home, no longer needing to spend months deployed, waiting for action. The salary tripled her current one, and the bonus structure with corporate stock and cash held great appeal. A month away from her re-enlistment date, she signed the contract and finished her term in the military.

Some days she missed the camaraderie that came with her enlistment but the freedom to come home when the job ended outweighed that in her mind. With this new job, she would get an assignment, go straight into the action, and then return safely home, like now.

Her mother wrapped her up in a gentle embrace. Emma inhaled the familiar smell of cloves she always associated with her and hugged her tight. "I had to pull over and rest for a little while."

Clicking her tongue, her mom said, "I knew you should have broken the trip up more."

"I never would have been able to rest. I wanted to get home." She hooked her arm through her mom's and steered her toward the back of the car. "Now, before I walk in to some big surprise party to celebrate getting out of the Army and act completely surprised, tell me who's here."

Her mom chuckled and said, "Your brother. School finished for him Friday, so he came home yesterday."

Emma smiled, thinking about her little brother Abel. He didn't remember Afghanistan at all. His first memories were when their family moved into this house right before his fourth birthday.

"Who else?" She pulled her stuffed duffel bag out of the trunk.

"Uncle Ivan and Aunt Rashida."

Emma gasped. "What are they doing here?" Her Uncle Ivan had come to Afghanistan with the Russian army, a young orphan barely eighteen. When his unit returned home, he defected and hid in her grandparents' home. Five years later, he married Zara's sister. They had a leather tooling shop in Ghazni. He was the first to recognize Emma's penchant for language and taught her Russian and what English he knew.

"They are thinking of moving here. Your baba is helping them."

Once they moved to the United States, her father embraced the lifestyle here. He enjoyed the cultural diversity and the energy. He loved pop culture and fast food. His enthusiasm for their new home spread to Emma and Abel. He made every day exciting and adventurous. He would love to bring all of their family to the States. "I haven't seen them since I was overseas about four months ago."

"It's been much longer for me."

She put her arm around her mother's shoulders. "I know." Instead of going to the party inside, she looked up and down the tree-lined street. How different this little neighborhood outside of San Antonio was compared to their home in Afghanistan!

Emma still remembered the day-to-day life there and the culture shock she experienced when she came to America. Everything was brighter, shinier, more colorful here. It was also busier and louder. She remembered her mom coming home from work, complaining about the way their family had been sucked into the busy fray of American life, missing the routine and comfort of her home. After she became a follower of Christ and learned what it looked like to be active in an American church, she began to love it here as much as her husband, especially once as she made friends and settled in.

"Ready?" her mom asked.

She turned and smiled, then grabbed the handle of her duffel bag and walked to the front door. She remembered coming here for the first time, running through the big, empty house with the shining hardwood floors, amazed that the whole thing was for just her family.

She opened the door and stepped inside as the people waiting yelled, "Surprise!"

Grinning, she tossed her duffel to the base of the stairs

and entered the front room. She reached her brother first. "Hello, Abel. I missed you."

"And I you." He hugged her. "So, no more Army? I'm surprised."

"Yeah. Me, too. God is leading me in a different way. I can't wait to tell you about it."

Her father approached with his arms wide. She said, "Baba!" He enveloped her in a hug and kissed the top of her head.

"I'm so proud of you."

Happy tears filled her eyes. "Thank you. That means a lot."

She worked her way through the room, talking to different people from her home church, her aunt and uncle and their daughter. Her mom brought out so much food from the kitchen that she wondered how the tables held it all. She told stories, answered questions, and soaked up the love and friendship in the room.

Hours later, she sat with her mom, dad, and brother at the little table in the kitchen. Their friends had left, and Ivan and Rashida had gone to bed to sleep off their jet lag. A steaming pot of tea sat in the center of the table within easy reach. Her father leaned over and rubbed her shoulder. "So, Emma, what's next for you?"

Of all the people in that house today, her father would be the most likely to understand the kind of work she'd been doing. She spoke five languages fluently and was working on learning a sixth. Between her translation skills and her tactical debriefing training, she was very much in demand in several hot spots around the world. That often placed her in dangerous situations. No father relished his daughter experiencing war of any kind.

"There's a company that contracts out the type of work I've been doing with the Army," she said. "I would almost have my pick of locations, but it wouldn't be months and months at a time. It would be weeks here and weeks there."

Her mom's face fell. "Back overseas?"

She reached over and covered her hand. "Sometimes. But also stateside."

Abel refreshed his mom's tea and said, "I think it's great. You can make a lot more money doing the same work."

Emma appreciated his support. "Yes. And I wouldn't be carrying a gun to do it." She laughed. "Or having to do PT at five in the morning. Plus, assignments would be my choice and not my orders."

Her father stood and put his cup and saucer in the sink. "God has been good to us. Coming here, living this life. I'm proud of you for serving this country. Our country." He looked around the table at his family. Emma could read the emotion in his eyes. "I am very thankful for you all," he said.

She had a hard time putting into words how much she missed her family when she was away from them. Here, she felt complete. They understood her and loved her. She felt like she could sit with these three people at this table and say anything; they'd listen and understand. She lifted her tea cup as if it were a toast in agreement with her father.

★ ★ ★

The light shifted on the page, and Emma looked up, frowning at the dark cloud that suddenly obscured the bright sun. As the breeze picked up and the temperature started dropping, she wondered how long she'd have until the storm forced her off this bench and inside.

She looked down at her book. A drop of rain plopped into the center of the paragraph she was reading. Resigned to having to give up the perfect bench spot, she stood and slipped her bag over her shoulder.

Right now, just before a downpour, the River Walk in San Antonio had very little foot traffic. Clearly, the storm had shown impending signs she'd ignored while escaping into her book. She had a choice: get drenched in a downpour that was seconds away or find a sanctuary from the deluge and flee to it. She looked around and spotted a tea house. Maybe she could grab a corner table and keep reading while she indulged in an afternoon snack.

Just as she stepped under the awning, the sky let loose. She smiled to herself at the perfect timing. When she entered the little cafe, the aroma of exotic and spicy teas warred with freshly baked pastries. She waited near the hostess stand, examining the shelf of offered teas and deciding she would order the hibiscus.

"Selah?"

She recognized the voice. As she turned, she spotted a familiar pair of eyes, but it took her a few seconds before recognition dawned. Lieutenant Jorge Peña. The last time she'd seen him had been from the deck of a container ship in the middle of the Arabian Sea six months ago. Then, he had a full beard, somewhat worse for wear combat boots, and a camouflage uniform along with heavy combat gear.

Today, he wore new climbing shoes, clean khaki cargo pants, and an expensive looking name brand collared golf shirt. She could make out his thickly muscled chest and arms beneath the shirt. His impressive biceps stretched the sleeves. He was also freshly shaved, which made him appear younger, more approachable, and—along with his apparel—considerably more attractive.

A burst of happiness at this unexpected encounter from someone from her previous life caused a smile to cover her face. "Lieutenant," she said warmly, stepping toward him, "what are you doing here?"

He gestured at the downpour outside, and she suddenly remembered droplets of sea water glistening in the tight curls of his dark hair when they were aboard that ship.

She held up her book, still keeping an index finger in her spot. "Same. I'd found the perfect bench. The storm snuck up on me."

The hostess appeared. "How many?"

Emma glanced at Peña, and he smiled in a way that made her heart skip a beat. He focused on the hostess and said, "Two, please." At her sudden grin, his eyes widened a little. "Sorry. It's okay, right?"

"*Si*," she answered quickly. "*Perfecta*."

Perhaps without realizing he had shifted to Spanish at her prompting, he nodded and quietly murmured, "*Espléndido.*"

Soon, they sat across from each other, steaming teapots at their elbows.

He sat up straight as if on the verge of a tremendously important announcement. "You're not Hispanic."

He said it as if it were a statement but she knew it was a question. She considered teasing him but let the idea go. "I never claimed to be Hispanic."

"Could never tell by hearing you speak Spanish. Your accent is perfect. You could pass easy."

Emma just nodded. She could pass for a number of ethnicities with only minor changes to her appearance.

Peña continued, "Where are your people from?"

"Texas by way of Afghanistan," she explained. "You?"

"A little town in northern Mexico called Los Angeles, California. Heard of it?" He smiled a toothless smile and waggled his eyebrows.

Emma hadn't realized he had a sense of humor. "Northern Mexico, huh? What brings you to San Antonio here in the heart of the Republic of Texas?"

She could tell he appreciated her repartee. "I've been here for two weeks on TDY for some training. You?"

"I'm from here. This is what you might call my home town." She smiled at the waitress, who set a tiered tray in the center of the table. Little crust free sandwich triangles filled the bottom tier, and the two remaining tiers held pastries and fruit. She then set a rather large bowl of fresh

Pico de Gallo between them and a covered basket of tortilla chips.

"Thought you were still stationed at Huachuca." Peña took two sandwiches and a scone, then poured tea into his cup. "You on leave?"

"No. That's right. I was at Huachuca." She took a sip of her tea. The hibiscus was as amazing as she'd imagined. "I got out about three months ago."

His eyelids lowered as he considered that information. Here, in this environment, away from enemies and danger, she noticed the golden flecks in his brown eyes. At first, she wondered why she'd never noticed them before, then why she noticed them now.

"Like, 'out' out?" He tore one of the triangles in half and popped the bite into his mouth. After he swallowed, he asked, "What are you doing for work now?"

"I'll be contracting pretty soon. Mainly I'll be working as a translator for the DOD."

He stared at her as if he could learn everything about her if he just looked at her long enough. "Just translating? No more than that? Seems like a waste of your other, uh, skills."

She thought about her abilities in the area of tactical debriefing. She had a unique talent for digging into someone's background and pulling out what she needed to convince him to talk. She could study a man's life, determine what mattered, and use it to gain an advantage. "Well, that kind of work doesn't necessarily get contracted out."

He lifted one shoulder in a casual shrug. "You get put with the right team, it won't matter."

"It would if I broke laws. That's not something I do." Foregoing cucumber and cream cheese, she dove right into the custard-filled puff pastry. Her eyes closed briefly at the wonderful flavor. She swallowed and said, "Besides, this will be easier work for more money."

"Sure. But where's the fun in easy?"

His grin was infectious and she couldn't help but return it. "When do you go back to Bragg?"

He sighed. "See? We were having this nice, polite conversation. You had me all disarmed by your feminine charms, then you start dropping cuss words."

She giggled at the idea of Fort Bragg being considered a cuss word. Most Special Operators had a love-hate relationship with Fort Bragg. Usually, they loved the training and hated the location. However, if you spent any amount of time under a green beret, you had to spend some time there. "Sorry. When must you return to the 'center of the universe'?"

The U.S. Army's John F. Kennedy Special Warfare Center and School at Fort Bragg was often called the "hub of the wheel" by green berets. Her reference to it as the universe's center earned a little appreciative bark of laughter. His teeth looked very white when he smiled. "Training ends tomorrow then I head back to the 'center of the universe' the day after. No one can escape its pull."

His face turned more serious and he said, "Wish I'd known you were here. And that this is your town. We could have got together so you could show off all your favorite places. Plus show off more of that feminine charm."

Wait. Feminine charms? That was the second time he'd said that. Was he flirting? Were they flirting? The idea made her heart flutter. The idea of spending time alone with him showing off her home town made her feel all squishy inside. What was wrong with her today?

He was probably here with the entire team. That's what he meant. He meant she could have played tour guide for the team. "Is it just you, or are you with the team?"

"Just me."

Oh.

Emma took a small bite of pastry and washed it down with some tea. She watched him munch on several heaping tortilla chip loads of Pico de Gallo and decided she liked the way he appreciated the meal.

She'd hadn't thought of Peña very much since she got into a helicopter on the deck of that ship. When she had written her report, she'd even had to look up his name. So, where did this sudden burst of disappointment at the fact that he'd been here for two weeks and she hadn't known come from? "I would have enjoyed that," she finally said. Low heat filled her cheeks. "I love San Antonio."

"I've been here a few times before. Toured the Alamo the first time I came." He looked around, then held up his delicate tea cup that somehow looked far too small for his fingers. He held his pinkie finger in the air and took a refined sip. "Never had afternoon tea before, though."

She chuckled. "Thank you, God, for rain."

"Amen."

They chatted about the team, about Fort Bragg, and touched briefly on the political climate.

"Do you still have family in Afghanistan?"

"I do." She thought about her aunt and uncle, who were still in San Antonio visiting her parents. Their visas would expire soon and they'd have to go back. "My father would like to wrap everyone up and bring them here. But, many of them don't want to leave."

"It's their home."

She set aside her empty cup and saucer and propped her chin in her hand. "Where's home for you, now, Lieutenant?"

"Jorge."

She raised an eyebrow. "Jorge? Where's that?"

His expression turned serious. "No. My name. It's Jorge. You're a civilian now. No need for that Lieutenant stuff."

"All right." She put on a mischievous grin. "Where's home for you now, Jorge? Bragg?"

He barked a little laugh again. "Definitely not Fort Bragg." In Spanish, he said, "You say my name like you know how to pronounce it properly."

She replied in his language. "That's because I do."

He sat back and said, "Yeah, so, still Los Angeles, I guess. But I haven't been there for many years. I moved to Arizona for college. Haven't been back to L.A. since then."

"At all?"

"Nothing there worth going back for. Don't want to sound like a cliché, but you could say the Army is my home, until I get out anyway." He looked around the little cafe. "What about you? You said you're from here?"

"I am. My parents still live in the house they first moved into when they came from Afghanistan."

"When did they come here?"

"In 2002." She paused, remembering the frantic packing and the American soldiers who were so kind to her on the transport to the air base. "My father helped America in late 2001. It put a target on his back." She could still hear her mom crying in the middle of the night and her father's quiet voice as he comforted her. She never once let on to Emma or Abel how scared she actually felt. She shrugged, meeting his eyes again. "We had to leave."

Emotion filled his eyes and a muscle ticked in his jaw. "Your father must be very brave."

Wanting to rid the heaviness that suddenly descended, she smiled a closed-lipped smile and wiggled her eyebrows. "Larger than life."

When the waitress returned with the check, Emma started to reach for it, but Jorge took it first. He slipped some cash into the folder and said, "My treat. I'm on per diem after all."

"Next time is on me, then," she said.

"I'll take you up on that now that you're a rich contractor." He checked his phone and said, "Unfortunately, I have to go. Wish I could stay. That Pico is good."

They stood together, and Emma picked up her book and bag. "I'm so happy we ran into each other," she said with sincerity.

"Me, too." They walked through the little cafe and out into the muggy afternoon. The storm clouds had passed, and the Texas sun resumed its vigil. Jorge glanced up at the sky then back at her. "I have two more days here. I'd love to see you again."

He would? She searched his face. He wasn't just being polite. He *was* flirting!

"I'd like that." She pulled her phone out of her bag, unlocked it, and held it out. "Send yourself a text so you have my number."

After he handed it back to her, he started to walk away. About three steps out, he turned and walked backward while he said, "Okay if I call you?"

She laughed and held up her hand in a wave. "Do it."

She watched him get into his rental car and drive away. She was halfway to her car when she realized she still had a silly grin covering her face.

CHAPTER

★

THREE

Camp Lemonnier near the Horn of Africa

Two Years Later

Heat waves danced above the packed dirt road. Emma strolled down the familiar alley, enjoying the feel of the hot African sun beating down on her bare arms. She'd just arrived from Poland. As much as she loved the beauty of the area around Poznań and Zakopane, she could do without the cold, wet winter.

Excitement hummed down her spine, and a small smile came to her face. She had six months assigned to this unit at Norton's request. While she had enjoyed the freedom of coming and going for mission-specific assignments, staying with Norton and his team for six months sounded like paradise. After all, when she worked with Norton, she worked with Jorge Peña.

Their paths had crossed four or five times in the last two years. The longest stretch of time had been the two weeks she taught at his home duty station in Fort Bragg, North Carolina. They'd had dinner three times in those two weeks, seen two movies, and went bowling twice. Unfortunately, all those events had been in a group and never just one-on-one.

She had always liked him, but the time at Bragg had secured her feelings for him. Now to get him to make a move. What was he waiting for, anyway?

She found the building and pushed open the door, stopping in front of the Sergeant stationed at the desk. "Honest Abe," she greeted Sergeant Ibrahim, "how are you?"

He pushed the log sheet toward her and said, "Very well, Selah. It's good to see you." As soon as she logged in and he scanned her common access card, or CAC, he said, "Briefing room B."

She put her CAC back into its plastic lanyard holder and walked down the hall, glancing at the labels on the closed doors. She stopped at the briefing room door and took a deep breath, working on pushing thoughts of everything except her job to the back of her mind.

Feeling centered, she opened the door and stepped in, finding Captain Norton, First Lieutenant Peña, First Lieutenant Osbourne, Chief Warrant Officer Four Hanson, and Sergeant Sanders at the table with their commander, Colonel Jenkins.

Norton stood and greeted. "Selah. Glad you could come."

"I always come when you call, Daddy," she said with a smile. She pulled out a chair and said, "Colonel. Sorry I'm late. There was a slight delay in Germany."

"Delay? Yeah. It's called Ramstein," Norton agreed.

Jenkins gave Norton a good-natured look for the humor before he asked. "How long do we have you, Selah?"

"A hundred and eighty days, sir. Well, a hundred seventy nine, to be precise." She handed over the stapled orders she'd printed. "Looking forward to it. Been too long since I worked with Captain Norton and his team."

She glanced at Jorge, who looked at her with serious brown eyes. When their eyes met, he gave her a faint smile. She remembered the gold flecks in his eyes that had reflected the lights in the tea room and the strong cut of his jaw now covered by a dark beard.

"Six months is a good bit of time," Jenkins said. He pushed back from the table. "Captain, why not go ahead and fill Selah in from our meeting this morning."

"Sir."

After the door shut behind him, Norton said, "We have an active mission, and I thought it would be easier to just have you present than to constantly have to request you."

She smiled. "I always enjoy working with your team, Captain. I appreciate your confidence in me."

"Well, best for the best, right?" He stood. "I know you just landed so I'll take it easy on you."

Sanders chuckled. "You never say that to me, Daddy."

"Drumstick, I always go easy on you."

Chief Hanson kept his tone bone dry. "I'd hate to see hard."

Norton's red beard moved with his smile. He continued. "As you know, we are at the corner of one of the superhighways of commerce for the world. Djibouti's northern border is especially strategic. Besides petroleum products, about one tenth of the world's seaborne trade moves through the Red Sea, so our comrades in arms in the Navy are stretched a bit thin. Additionally, conventional forces including elements from the National Guard have performed multiple security operations in Katengala, Kenya, Somalia, and here in Djibouti."

Emma nodded during his pause. "Understood, sir."

Norton said, "Our macro mission is to identify, capture, and debrief individual bad actors in this region whether their motivation is piracy or terrorism. Once we finish with them, they can be dispatched according to our findings. We have met with limited success in the last thirty days. You are here to support that macro mission. You report directly to Colonel Jenkins and you are operationally

tasked to me. You're a vet, so you know how this works."
He studied her face for a few seconds. "It's late on the East
Coast and the SCIF is iffy right now, so first mission
specifics can wait until morning. You get settled into a
bunk yet?"

"Not yet sir, but I know where to go."

"That's right. You've been here a couple of times."

"Yes, sir."

"Well, get settled, unpacked. Join us at zero-eight in
our ready room and we'll get you read on." Norton stood,
followed by everyone else. "Glad to have you here. If you
need anything that isn't here, just ask."

"Thank you, sir."

"See that she gets some chow before tucking in, Peña."

"Sir, yes sir."

Soon, just she and Jorge remained. She smiled at him.
"How are you?" she asked.

"A little jet-lagged still." He visibly relaxed, leaning
back in his chair. "But, happy to see you," he said, his words
washing over her.

"It's always good to see you." She felt the heat in her
cheeks at her own boldness, but determined that if he
didn't make the next move, she would. "Have you eaten
lunch yet?"

"No. I'm headed there now." He stood and walked to
the door, and she quickly got to her feet to follow him.
Before he opened the door, he turned and faced her.
"Eleven minutes."

She knew exactly what he meant. Looking around, she

asked, "Your point?"

"We've never been alone in a secure room before, so I'm going to take this opportunity to ask you. We couldn't crack Haafiz Durrani. You stroll in and inform him that he'll talk within twenty minutes, and it took eleven. Never got to ask. What made you choose that tactic?"

With a slow smile, she stepped forward until the toes of her boots almost touched his. "Jorge, I would love to tell you. But what do I get in return?"

He started to open his mouth but then closed it, his eyes laughing even if his face gave no indication. "Well, Ms. Selah..."

"Doctor."

"I beg your pardon?"

"I have a Ph.D. If you're going to get formal with me, you may as well do it properly."

A small smile started to crack through his stoic face. "I apologize. *Doctor* Selah, you would get the satisfaction of schooling the intelligence officer of the most elite SFODA this fine military has to offer."

She looked him up and down, from the curly black hair and close-trimmed beard, down his fit torso, to his brown boots. When she met his eyes again, she said, "How about dinner?"

He raised both eyebrows and asked, "Dinner?"

"Yeah. Next time we're in the States, you take me to dinner. Last time we had plans you got called away, and we never had that dinner date, remember?"

The flush that covered his cheeks pleased her. "You

want to have dinner with me?"

Definitely. "I'd love to. Thanks for asking." She smiled as she stepped slightly back, wanting to give them both a little space. "There was no time. I had to lie. I convinced him that we'd nuke Mecca in retaliation and made that something he believed. He absolutely thought I had the authority and power to do it, too."

He crossed his arms over his chest. "How did you know he'd believe it?"

"First, my historical knowledge of al-Masjid al-Ḥarām, the Great Mosque, and especially of the seizure back in December of 1979 gave him the idea that I had the authority. But really, I read his file. No father. His Syrian mother led a terrorist cell in Northern Afghanistan even when it wasn't cool for women to do such things. I went in hard and demanding, and he complied. I would have shifted tactics if it didn't work."

He studied her for several moments before he said, "That feels too easy."

"Oh, Pina Colada, there's nothing easy about it." She gestured at the door. "Lunch?"

Jorge looked at the clock on the wall of the ready room and sighed. Two-twenty-two. He hated jet lag. He would love it if someone designed a way of travel that didn't kick him in the teeth coming and going.

He'd brought his laptop with him tonight, hoping to prep for tomorrow's briefing, but he had difficulty focusing on the mission. Instead, thoughts of Emma Selah kept infiltrating, pushing dossiers and mission objectives way to the back of his mind.

Which was why, when she walked into the room, he almost didn't believe she was actually there. He thought he was imagining it.

She'd contained her long black hair in a braid that fell over one shoulder. She wore a pair of gray sweatpants and a New York Yankees T-shirt. When she saw him, she paused, smiled, and headed for the refrigerator.

"Wow," he said. "You just stroll in here wearing an enemy uniform."

"Oh. Don't tell me. Dodgers fan."

"Not really. My favorite team is whoever's playing the Yankees." He didn't even crack a smile. "What's wrong with the Rangers, anyway?"

"Nothing. Love the Rangers. But the Astros are my team. They're about two hundred miles closer to home. The shirt was a gift."

"Some gift," he snorted.

"Can't sleep?" she asked as she pulled out a water bottle.

"Jet lag." He shut the lid of his computer and set it on the table in front of him. "You?"

"I slept. Then..." She paused, then pointed at her temple and a circling motion with her finger. "...dreams. Always hard to come to this part of the world."

She said that like he'd know what she meant. In a way he did, but he didn't think his experiences were the same as hers. "Why?"

She climbed onto the couch and crossed her legs under her. "Don't you remember that I come from Afghanistan?"

His eyes widened. "That's right. You were what, ten? Definitely old enough to remember the war." After a brief pause, he softly added, "It must have been hard for you to see the recent American retreat."

Tears filled her eyes but she blinked them back. "It was horrible. Everything we worked so hard for. Thankfully, my family got out. But it took every connection and influence my father had to do it." She paused, then shook her head. "Anyway, do you still have family in Los Angeles?"

Unbidden, his mind immediately put him in one of the eleven foster homes he'd lived in. He shook his head. "Nope." Then he smiled. "No family other than this team. They're my family."

She studied his face. "It's a good family to have."

After a few silent moments, he said, "Tell me about these dreams that keep you awake."

"They aren't that interesting. They just make me not want to go back to sleep." She shifted so she could prop her elbow on the arm of the couch. "When we fled to America, it was very dangerous. My dad's brother sacrificed himself so that we could get away. Even at ten, I understood everything that was happening."

"That would be hard to process all that at such a young age." He couldn't imagine the terror her family had gone through. "Why did you choose languages?"

With a casual shrug she said, "I spoke four languages pretty fluently by age ten. Farsi, Arabic, Russian, and English. Then I took Spanish in high school."

"*Tú hablas español? Fluida?*"

"*Si.*" She grinned. "Probably as well as you."

With a chuckle he doubtfully scoffed, "*Lo dudo.*" His grin softened the rebuke. "But I have no doubt you speak better Russian and Arabic."

She toyed with the end of her braid. "Languages came easy. When I joined the Army, they put me in the Human Intelligence Collector Course because of my language skills. Studying linguistics in college just made sense. Since getting out of the Army, I've finished my Ph.D. in linguistics." She tilted her head as if to look at him from a different angle. "Wait a second. You speak Arabic, don't you?"

"Some. And not very well," He thought about his time at the Defense Language Institute. "I understand what I hear more than I can speak it with fluency. But when I'm in a situation where I'm immersed, that really knocks the rust off."

"Total immersion is how I learned French."

"Has your last name always been Selah, or did you change it in the States?"

"No, it's a family name. I love it. In Arabic, it means righteous."

Jorge grinned an ironic grin. "My last name means grief."

She searched her mind. "I thought it meant pineapple."

He shook his head. "Different spelling."

"Huh. Righteous and grief." She shifted to stand. "I think I can sleep some more, now. Thanks for the conversation."

He sat quietly long after she'd gone. He couldn't believe he'd agreed to go to dinner with her.

As much as the idea appealed to him, it wouldn't be appropriate to date her. There were lots of reasons. The reasons began with the fact that they worked closely together in a war zone and went on from there all the way up to one very big reason. The reason he'd canceled their dinner date in Texas and left a day early, and the reason he always encouraged group gatherings when she was with their team.

There were less important reasons. She wasn't Hispanic, not that it really mattered that much to him. But they didn't share that culture, heritage, or past. And the fact that he was Hispanic might matter a great deal to her family. He had no idea.

If he could go back to yesterday, he'd have left with Norton and not had the impulse to engage her about Haafiz Durrani. But the way she'd handled that debriefing two years ago had impressed him, and his professional curiosity had gotten the better of him. Every time he'd seen her since, by chance or design, circumstances had never allowed them the privacy or venue for that conversation. Finding himself in a secure room, alone with her, had been too much of a temptation.

While they had that time alone, he should have found

some way to share a very real truth about himself with her. It was not very important to him, but he suspected it might be important to her. At least, if things kept going the way he saw them going.

With a sigh, he rubbed his eyes. Maybe she'd forget about dinner once they were all back in the States. Then none of it would matter.

CHAPTER

★

FOUR

The rumble of the engines of a C-130 blew past them. Everyone paused as the noise drowned out the hope of conversation. As soon as the noise faded, the Colonel shifted toward her and rubbed at his white beard. "Just how many languages do you speak, Selah?"

"Six, sir. I'm working on Hebrew, hoping to make it seven."

"Here I only speak two. English and bad English," the Colonel said. He pushed a file toward her. "This particular gentleman claims he doesn't speak Arabic. Look familiar?"

She opened the folder and skimmed the first page. A photo of a man with leathery brown skin and light brown eyes that sat behind bushy white eyebrows was stapled to the top of the page. She recognized the name but not the face. "If he's actually from Bamiyan, he likely speaks Farsi," she said, imagining the mountain village in Afghanistan. "Has anyone tried?"

"Don't know yet. We just have what the agency sent us."

Norton said, "Our friends in the State Department have him at a secure location about two hundred kilometers away. They've requested we perform the tactical debrief on this guy because of our recent intimate knowledge of the doings in this region."

Jorge clicked some keys on the keyboard in front of him and a series of faces filled a grid on the wall. "He's a lieutenant in the Punjabi group, one of nine we know of. We need to find out what their next target is. CIA grabbed him as part of a different mission, so their people don't know what to ask him."

She flipped through the file and grabbed as much new information as possible in the few seconds she took. She would study it thoroughly later. "When do we leave?"

"Zero eight." Colonel Jenkins pushed back from the table and stood, effectively ending the meeting. "Team will escort you. You got gear?"

"Yes, sir." She looked up from the file. "I'll need comms. I prefer to borrow them from the unit I'm with instead of trying to integrate my own."

"Morita or Gill will get you rigged up on our comms," Norton assured.

★★★

As her opponent swept her feet out from under her, he simultaneously hit her square in the chest, and Emma went flying. She landed hard on her back with a grunt but immediately flipped her legs up and pulled them under her so she could stand. Then she lifted her gloved fists and smiled.

Sergeant First Class Wade "Commando" Chandler swiped at his black beard and rocked forward on the balls of his feet. "You have to use your brain because you'll never have the size advantage," he reminded her. "I'm bigger. I'm stronger. Disarm me? Don't care. Let's face it. I could kill you with my bare hands. What else can you do?"

She danced around him, testing the spring in the mat. She stepped a little closer and raised her left arm as if she was about to swing at him, but at the last second jumped up and kicked, swinging her leg hard. The side of her foot hit him in the side of his head, and he staggered back. The second she had both feet on the ground, she jumped again and delivered a side kick low to his chest. He fell backward.

For a moment, he lay still. She rushed forward. "You okay?"

"I'm good," he panted. "Solar plexus. Knocked the wind out of me."

She pulled her glove off and held out a hand, helping

him to his feet. He towered over her by a good six inches. "Nice," he said, unstrapping his helmet. "You've been practicing."

She and Wade had sparred together since just after Basic Training twelve years ago. He'd gone on to active duty. She'd stayed in the Reserves until she finished her second three-year commitment. She liked fighting with him. He was a happily married man with a little boy and never tried to make their relationship anything other than friendship.

"I joined a gym."

"Where are you now?"

"Dallas. Moved there two years ago. I have an apartment I see only a few weeks a year, but the location saves a layover in the flight or long-term parking fees." She walked off the mat and tossed the gloves into her bag. "What about you? I saw Allison's posts about the bakery in New York City."

His blue eyes softened at the mention of his wife. "We closed on it before I left, but she's still at her parents' in Charleston." He pulled two bottles of water out of his bag and tossed one to her. "I've done everything I can do on my end. Just biding my time until this deployment is over, and then I'll be thanking Uncle Sam for the years and the college money and finish that last semester of culinary school."

"Well, congratulations. I know this has been your dream for a while."

"Long as I can remember."

The door opened. Norton entered with Sergeant Bill "Drumstick" Sanders. When he saw her, his face lit up. "'Who is this King of glory? The LORD of hosts, He is the King of glory. Selah.'"

With a smile, she said, "Selah," along with him.

He nodded and grinned. "Good to see you, twenty-four-ten." Norton quoted Psalms 24:10 just about each time he saw her after a long absence and he had christened her with twenty-four-ten as her unofficial callsign.

"Likewise, Daddy. Drumstick, how's your day going?" His charm and whit made it fun to work with him. Added to that, she'd never met anyone who could read facial expressions and body language like Sanders. His presence definitely gave her an advantage in a tactical debriefing. They'd developed a code with microphone clicks that they used whenever he accompanied her into a room. "Me? I'm just dandy like a 'possum eatin' a sweet tater."

He exaggerated his Alabama accent when he said that. Before she could respond, the door opened, and Jorge walked in. He had wireless earbuds in his ears and looked down at the MP3 player in his hand. He walked past them without looking up.

In the last week, the only time he'd spoken to her was for direct mission-oriented information.

Wade watched him walk away. "Looks like we got a morning briefing."

"Or he found the long-lost ABBA album," Sanders said. "Could go either way."

Emma slung the strap of her bag over her shoulder and

said, "Thanks for the workout, Commando. Daddy, Drum, see you 'round."

She spun on her heel and rushed after Jorge, catching him as he set his bag on the floor beside a treadmill. She touched the back of his arm and stepped back, giving him room to realize who had touched him. As soon as he saw her, he hit a button on the player and popped the earbuds out. "Selah. Hi." He gestured at the treadmill. "Did you want this machine?"

"Nope." She set her bag next to his and asked, "Do you have a problem with me being Afghani?"

He jerked his face back as if she'd slapped him. "What? What does that mean?"

"I don't know." She refused to feel nervous about having this conversation. He'd been acting cool to her, and she hadn't done anything to deserve it. "Since I've been here, you've barely spoken to me."

He raised an eyebrow. "I've been *busy* since the day we spoke in private." He'd had seven strategic meetings and conducted one rather precarious mission since then, but didn't shed light on those specifics.

"So have I. Not the point. Whenever you've seen me, you've said only what you have to say and nothing more. So what's up with that? I thought we had a friendship forming."

"Oh." He took a deep breath and said, "I don't think a friendship with you is appropriate considering our business relationship." She watched his eyes as he spoke. He started to look down but pulled back at the end. Why was he not telling her the truth? She waited to see if he would elaborate. Finally, he added, "It's just not a good idea."

She shouldn't have pushed him. She should have let this growing thing between them move at its natural pace. Irritation tightened the muscles in her neck. She took a step backward. "I don't really think that's your reason, but I'll leave it be. Sorry to bother you, Lieutenant."

As she spun around, he grabbed her arm. She froze, contemplating whether to shrug off his touch, and decided against it. Instead, she looked pointedly at the hand that still gripped her arm then at him. He released her and said, "I do like you, Selah. I wish I could take it further. I think about you...." He stopped speaking abruptly. More slowly, he said, "I think about you a lot."

She gasped, not expecting such an admission. "We seem to be in the same predicament," she said with more boldness than she felt. "Maybe God's speaking."

In Spanish, he said, "*Lo dudo.*" I doubt it.

"Are you in love with someone back home or something? Got a girl at Bragg?"

With a frown that brought his eyebrows together, he said, "No. That's not it."

She crossed her arms over her chest. "Then I would like to get to know you more, possibly see what happens between us. I'm here for six months. We've never had more than two weeks. If it doesn't work out, I promise to keep interrogating prisoners for you."

He returned her smile, sighed, and rubbed the back of

his neck. "You are as good at getting someone to do something as you are at getting information, aren't you?"

"Only when it's important to me."

After several moments, he looked like he was on the verge of saying something different but he finally said, "Fine."

He didn't elaborate, so she grinned and said, "Fine? That's it?"

"What more do you want?"

She looked around and hopped up onto the treadmill next to his. "I guess I'll take fine." She hit the button to turn it on and started going at a slow jog. She looked over at him. He just stood there. He looked like he had something more to say but he couldn't figure out exactly how. Had she pushed him too hard? What if he was trying to figure out some way to back out? She really didn't want him to take it back.

She didn't know what else to say so she asked, "Weren't you going to go running?"

He glanced back at the treadmill. "Yeah." He got on the treadmill and looked over at her again. She met his eyes. After he turned his machine on, he asked, "What does this look like, then?"

She pressed the up arrow to increase her pace. "Don't know. New territory." When the setting felt right, she focused on keeping her feet hitting the belt at the right rhythm. "Looking forward to learning, though."

CHAPTER

★

FIVE

Exhaustion clawed at the back of Jorge's neck as he watched Emma through the monitor. She worked on the prisoner for the second hour while Sanders stood guard in the room, communicating with her through clicks in the microphone as he spotted subtle nuances in the way the prisoner's expression and body language changed.

Norton kicked back in the chair and put his feet up on the corner of the table. They'd been awake for pushing forty hours.

"What do you think?" his captain asked.

Jorge considered the determined look on the prisoner's face. "I think our intel was good. Drumstick seems confident. I can hear the clicks and they're getting more frequent. She's wearing him down."

The phone on the table next to Norton's phone rang. He sighed. "I bet you an ice water that's the spooks wanting an update."

Jorge shook his head. "No bet." He grabbed the receiver. "CJSOTF-HOA holding area. Lieutenant Peña speaking. May I help you sir or ma'am?"

"Lieutenant Peña, Carmine Olsten. Do we have a status?"

He pictured the tall man with long gray hair. As he started to speak, he watched the change in dynamics on the screen. "Standby," he said, shifting the receiver away from his ear and sat forward. The prisoner covered his face with his hands, his shoulders shaking. Emma sat forward, getting closer to him, speaking rapidly in Farsi. When he fisted his hand and slammed it on the table, Sanders moved swiftly and grabbed him by the back of the neck, pushing his head down until his cheek lay on the table. Selah bent low, the silk of her scarf brushing against his nose, and continued to speak. Finally, he started talking.

She gradually sat back, nodding, listening, interjecting, then stood and gestured for Sanders to release him. Norton had turned up the sound. He heard her order the prisoner to be taken to his room and given food and water.

Jorge put the phone back up to his ear. "Looks like the

debriefer just got something. Does she have your contact info?"

"She does. I'd like it soon. I don't need a complete report. Just the Cliff's notes for now."

When the call disconnected without warning, Jorge looked at the receiver and said, "Oh yeah, you have a nice day, too, *sir.*"

"Spooks." Norton observed redundantly. "You owe me an ice water."

Before Jorge could protest that he had not accepted the wager, Emma came in.

"I'll take one, too," Emma said as she entered the room.

She pulled the scarf off her head and wearily sank into the chair next to Jorge. He wanted to tell her how proud he was of her work in there, but didn't know how to word it so that she understood what he meant. Instead, he said, "Less than two hours. I think the pool was sitting at three, minimum."

Norton snorted. "I would have given you an hour. A little surprised it took you so long."

"Yeah, well, maybe I'm slowing down in my old age."

He stood and said, "Oh, that's right. Happy birthday."

The grin that covered her face did funny things to Jorge's pulse. "Thank you, sir."

"Now, hit the sack," Norton said on his way out. "We've earned a day off tomorrow."

She dabbed at the edge of the dark makeup surrounding her eye. He barely recognized her with the dark liner. "I'm starving. Do you think the chow hall is still open?"

Jorge shook his head. "Closed an hour ago."

She stuck her bottom lip out in a pout. "Sad. Do you think the ready room has anything I can snack on?" The phone rang and she frowned at it. "I guess I better get the report written so they'll let me go to bed," she murmured. As she picked up the receiver, she hit some buttons on the keyboard. The monitored room went away and a file directory appeared. "CJSOTF-HOA holding area. Emma Selah speaking. May I help you sir or ma'am?" she asked, clicking her mouse and opening an appropriate file. After a pause, she said, "I need ten minutes." Another pause then, "Roger. Wilco."

When she hung up, Jorge said, "Why don't I go get the sandwiches I grabbed for us before they closed? I had a feeling you wouldn't eat before you went in there. You can do your report and then shut down and relax."

"You're wonderful." She glanced at him as she started typing. "Thank you for thinking of me."

"Of course," he said. He squeezed her shoulder on his way out of the room.

He left the building and double-timed it to his unit's ready room. In the wake of their mission, no one was in the building. He imagined everyone had gone to bed already. He opened the fridge and found the sandwiches and cupcake he'd stored there. He'd left sticky notes on the food so that no one would take them.

Back in the headquarters building, he found Selah still typing. She glanced up when he entered the room and said,

"One more paragraph." A few seconds later, she hit the ENTER key on the keyboard and sat back. "Done!"

He handed her a turkey with provolone on sourdough, and she grinned at him. "I appreciate your foresight."

As she bit into the sandwich, he looked at the clock. "Only ten minutes left of your birthday."

"Definitely not one for the celebratory records, was it?"

"Oh, I don't know." He opened his own sandwich and said, "There was lots of fireworks and loud noises."

She put her hand over her mouth as she started to laugh. "I can't believe I laughed at that."

He winked and pulled the plastic container out of his pocket. He set the little cupcake down beside her plate. "Best eat this before midnight."

The grin on her face lit up her eyes, lit up his heart. "Oh, Jorge. Thank you." She started to open it, then paused and said, "You're not going to sing, are you?"

"Yeah, no." He picked up the triangular half of the sandwich and ate a third of it with one bite. "No one wants that."

She set her sandwich aside for the cupcake. He completely respected that decision. She took a small bite and closed her eyes as if savoring the sweet chocolate. When she opened them again and caught her staring at her, she asked, "Would you like a bite?"

"No, thanks," he said softly.

"I love the western celebration of birthdays, mainly because I love cake," she said, licking her fingers.

"How did you celebrate your birthday in Afghanistan?"

She shrugged. "We didn't. It's not a thing."

"Interesting."

"Birthday celebrations are all about the birth of Christ. You light candles because Christ was the light of the world. You eat sweet cake because his is the sweetest name. You exchange presents because the wise men brought him gifts. All of it is tradition around the birth of Christ and I only came to know Christ after I came to the US."

He'd never heard anything like that before. He studied her face. She had slight shadows under her eyes. He imagined he did as well. It had been a long two days. His exhaustion had lowered his defenses. When she slowly licked some chocolate frosting off her finger, he surged to his feet, wanting to leave before he did or said something both of them weren't ready for.

He tossed the sandwich wrapper in the trash can and asked, "Think you'll make it to chapel tomorrow?"

"At fourteen hundred?"

He nodded

She said, "Yes. I like the new chaplain."

"Good. See you tomorrow." He started from the room but paused, turned, and said, "Happy birthday, Emma. I hope this year is your best yet."

She smiled around a bite of cake and then swallowed. "It's already looking up."

★★★

They had the half-court basketball gym to themselves. The wood floor gleamed with polish and reflected fluorescent lights. Any noise they made echoed around the empty metal building.

Emma dribbled the basketball and started to move forward, but Jorge blocked her path. She pivoted and put her shoulder into pushing past him. He grunted at the impact but didn't budge.

"How does someone as short as you like playing basketball? Seems like you might prefer short people games like checkers or the limbo," he teased, moving like he was going to steal the ball out from under her. She watched his hips and anticipated the movement, then went in the opposite direction, shifting the ball to her other hand and getting past him.

As soon as she was free, she set up for the shot and sent the ball through the hoop. It made a satisfactory swishing sound as it whisked through the net.

"It doesn't take height," she said as he grabbed the ball and moved back to the center of the court. "Just mad skill."

He started forward, dribbling as he moved. She blocked him and he plowed into her. He let the ball go as he saved her from falling by wrapping her up in his arms. As soon as he released her, she started giggling as she went for the ball.

"Oh no you don't," he said, grabbing her and wrapping both arms around her.

"Personal foul! Personal foul!" She pretended to try to get free, but the laughter took the strength out of her arms. Instead, she let him turn her around. With his arms still around her, he looked down at her, a rare smile covering his face.

Her laughter gradually faded. With one arm around her waist, he reached out and brushed a strand of hair off her forehead, his touch gentle, almost caressing. She relaxed against him and cupped his cheek with her hand. His beard tickled her palm. "Jorge," she whispered, his name rolling off her tongue.

He glanced at her mouth, then back into her eyes. After years of a back-and-forth dance, was he finally going to kiss her?

Just as he lowered his head, his lips a breath above hers, the gym door crashed open. She immediately felt the change come over him as he straightened and slowly let her go. When she turned, she saw their chaplain walk in with a man in civilian clothes.

Slow heat flushed her cheeks at being caught in so intimate an embrace while in a hostile environment. She stepped back away from Jorge and rubbed the sides of her shorts with her hands.

"Lieutenant Peña," the chaplain said. "Captain Norton told me I might find you here."

He took another step away from her and asked, "What's up, sir?"

The chaplain looked at Emma and back at him. "Perhaps somewhere private?"

He glanced at her and said, "It's okay."

The chaplain cleared his throat, and his cheeks turned bright red. "I'm afraid I have some bad news. We just received word that Martina Gomez died this morning."

"How?" he asked, taking an unconscious step away from Emma.

"Who's Martina Gomez?" Emma asked quietly. Jorge never talked about his family. She was pretty sure he didn't have any family anymore.

Ignoring Emma, the chaplain explained, "Her company was assisting with a fire suppression effort in the Northwest and she, along with two others, were caught in a firestorm. I'm told they suffocated before the fire reached them."

Jorge glanced at Emma. Matter-of-factly, he said, "My wife."

Emma gasped. His wife?

His WIFE?

Jorge turned his attention back to the chaplain and mumbled, "I saw the reports on the fire in the news. Didn't know she was part of the relief. We haven't talked in a long time." Emma could see the muscle tick in his jaw, but he did not look at her again. Instead, he asked, "What do I need to do?"

The civilian spoke. "I'm Darrin Black, Lieutenant. I'm with the International Red Cross. If you come with me, I'll walk you through it."

Was she dreaming? Was that it? Some weird part of her psyche playing games with her?

When Jorge finally turned back to her, he looked like a kid's party balloon from which all the air had drained. She held up both hands and took a step back. "No."

"Hang on a sec, Emma," he said, his voice strangely

calm. He took a step back toward her. "Just let me..."

He had almost kissed her. She had almost let him kiss her. She had wanted him to kiss her!

"No!" Frantic, she looked from the chaplain to Jorge, unable to properly comprehend. Apparently, not a dream, or she'd have woken up screaming by now. "Don't say another word."

She spun on her heel and raced out of the gym.

By the time she hit the door, hot tears had filled her eyes. She had to get out of there before any of them saw her cry. Instead of running down the street, she just went around the building to the back. There, she leaned against the side of the building and put her hands around her stomach.

His wife?

Her mind raced through every conversation she'd had with him over the last two years. Never, not one single time, had he mentioned a wife or anyone by the name of Martina. Who else knew about this? Did the members of the team all sit around and laugh behind their hands at the gullible little Emma Selah while she let a married man have a deployment fling with her?

Soon, anger pushed the tears away. She swiped the tears off her face with impatient movements and pushed her shoulders back. "Fool me once, shame on you," she proclaimed through clenched teeth.

Calmer, she walked away from the gym and back to her quarters. As she passed the unit's ready room, Sanders came out. "Hey twenty-four-ten," he greeted as he put his hat on.

"Sergeant Sanders," she answered crisply. She did not stop or engage him. If he thought that out of character, he didn't say. Instead, she just kept going until she got to her room.

Thankfully, her DA Civilian bunkmate Claire wasn't there. She had LOC duty until twenty-two hundred tonight. Alone, away from any peering eyes or judgment, Emma threw herself onto her cot and covered the back of her head with her hands.

CHAPTER

SIX

It always felt weird to be back in Los Angeles. He didn't particularly enjoy it, but it was the city to which he felt the most connection.

Jorge stood on the cracked sidewalk and closed his eyes, feeling the dry grittiness born of exhaustion. He'd love to sleep, but every time he tried, all he could think about was the wrecked look on Emma's face. He should have followed her and explained. He should have made her hear him before he went away.

The Red Cross guy told him he could catch the hop leaving in twenty minutes or wait two days until the next one. Knowing the operational status of his unit and what was coming on their horizon, getting out of there two days earlier meant he could come back two days earlier. That was the smartest decision. But it left very little time to speak to Emma.

He'd knocked on her door, but she hadn't answered. He tried to send her an email, but he couldn't get connectivity once he was on the plane. Instead, he thought about the look on her face for the twenty hours it took him to travel from Djibouti to Los Angeles. On that flight, he decided to speak with her in person and not send a long, complicated email. Instead, he sent a simple one:

```
THERE IS AN EXPLANATION. I'LL
BE BACK IN TWO WEEKS. TRUST
ME.
```

He walked down the street where he'd lived with his grandmother, trying to pick the house from the dozen that looked identical to it. Their mother had abandoned him and his brother within hours of Jorge's birth. Their grandmother had done what she could, but she had worked two jobs her entire life—as a waitress by day and a janitor by night. What little retirement she had was not enough to raise two boys.

He could still remember the day the social worker came. He was six years old and his brother Julián was eight.

Their abuela had packed their belongings into paper grocery bags, labeling each with their names. Julián had known what she was doing and screamed profanities at her as they dragged him away. It was several days before Jorge realized he would never see her again.

Julián had joined a gang at thirteen. A social worker informed Jorge of his death three years later, leaving him completely alone in the world.

When he got a job, he went to tell his abuela that he could help care for her and provide for her. He planned to ask if he could move back to her home, but he could never find her again.

As if a fresh wound, his heart filled with the fear and grief he'd felt that day. Was it really fifteen years ago that he searched the houses on this street, despair filling him when he realized she was gone? It felt like it happened this morning.

Pushing the memories back, he returned to the street where he'd parked his car. Two gangsters leaned against the hood, watching him walk up. The tall, skinny one straightened and laughed. "Hey, *ese*," he said as his buddy crossed his arms over his broad chest. "You ready to pay the parking tax?"

Jorge took a slow, deep breath and stopped about two feet away. "Get away from my car," he said succinctly.

The skinny guy laughed. "Maybe you don't *hablo* English. You in my territory now, dude. You pay or you don't walk out of here."

Jorge shook his head. "I don't plan to walk. I plan to

drive. Last warning, *engañar*."

The broader chest guy snorted. "*Engañar*."

Tall skinny guy pulled a 9mm Beretta out of his waistband. "Empty your pockets, *ese*. This ain't no joke."

"No?" Before skinny guy could realize his intent, Jorge took the Beretta from him, breaking his wrist in the same movement. The skinny gangster grabbed his arm and fell to his knees, yelling.

Jorge dropped the magazine and emptied the chamber then disassembled the gun, dropping the spring, the slide, the compensator and so on directly onto the sidewalk pavement. He put the firing pin in his shirt pocket just seconds before the broad-chested guy finally stepped forward, a knife clutched in his right hand. He lunged at Jorge, who grabbed his wrist and brought his knee up into the guy's ribcage very fast. He twisted the guy's trapped wrist viciously, forcing him to drop the knife. His attacker fell forward, clutching his stomach, and Jorge brought the heel of his foot down hard on his temple, sending him all the way down struggling to stay conscious.

Jorge looked down at the tear-filled face of the skinny guy and asked, "So do I kill you? Or do you run away?"

Skinny didn't even look behind him at his friend. Instead, he stumbled forward onto his feet and ran down the road, cradling his broken arm to his chest.

The entire incident had taken less than a minute.

Annoyed, Jorge tossed the firing pin into his cup holder as he got into his car. Adrenaline pumped through his limbs, heightening his senses. He fisted his hands a couple of times, then drove quickly down the street and out of the neighborhood. A couple of miles away, he pulled into a shopping center, wanting the aggression simmering under his surface to cool down before driving into the complexity of Los Angeles traffic.

He glanced around the shopping center, his eyes resting on a Christian bookstore. He got out of his rental car, retrieved the firing pin from the cup holder, and strolled across the parking lot. He tossed the firing pin into a garbage can outside the store then strolled inside. When he entered the store, his first thought was how clean it smelled. He walked through the displays of kitchen utensils carved with Bible verses, past the children's section. Three little kids sat on beanbags watching a cucumber in a pirate hat sing on the screen.

He hadn't had a typical Christian upbringing, but a couple of his foster parents had taken him to church. The biggest impact on his spiritual life once he became an adult had come from Martina. One night during basic training, they both had duty overnight, and she told him about her God, the one who saved her from a life in the same gang that had eaten up and spat out his brother. Her sincerity radiated off of her like beams of light.

They became almost inseparable after that moment, and he started attending chapel services with her whenever they had the freedom to do so.

Both of them headed to intelligence school after that. They graduated and transitioned to becoming members of the United States Army National Guard. She told him about a full time job she'd gotten outside a military base in Arizona. He figured that was as good a place as any, and he followed her lead, filling out the interstate transfer requests for the National Guard and moved there, too.

While he went to college by day, he worked as a security guard for a jewelry store by night, giving him ample time to study. He and Martina went to church together, but didn't see much of each other until their unit deployed to Iraq.

The door to the store dinged as someone else came in. Jorge glanced in that direction, saw a woman with a little boy, then went back to browsing. He stopped when he saw the marriage display. The words, "in sickness and in health," caught his attention, taking him back to the day their convoy was attacked.

Martina had gotten shot in the neck. He couldn't believe she lived after all the blood she'd lost. He kept his hand on her neck through the transport to the hospital and only released her when the doctor insisted that he was in her way.

Two days later, he sat by her bed and they mourned the loss of a friend who died in the initial attack.

"He's like us, Jorge. He's got no one." Martina's voice was weak. Her skin had an ashen hue to it.

"We've got each other," he said softly.

"Won't matter if one of us bites it. Army won't give me leave to see you get a proper burial. 'Best friend' is not a classification they recognize."

He could see the panic in her eyes, the worry. "I could

adopt you," he said, trying to lighten the mood.

She'd closed her eyes and dozed off for about ten minutes. When she opened them again, she'd said, "Marry me."

He'd actually snorted. "You don't love me."

"No. And you don't love me. But I'm never planning on a relationship with anyone, and neither are you. We might as well be each other's someone. Take care of our bodies, our estates."

It had made sense to him at the time. He couldn't imagine ever wanting to share a life with anyone. He wanted to serve his country with honor and dignity, save money so that in retirement, he'd live a comfortable life far away from the smog that covered Los Angeles. Nothing else appealed to him as far as his future went.

They'd gotten married a month later by a Sierra Vista, Arizona judge. The one and only time they kissed was for the sealing of the deal in front of witnesses who they never met before or since. They'd gone from the courthouse to the Army's personnel division and registered each other as spouses. They made new wills, signed life insurance policies, then went to their own homes that night.

It was weird, this marriage of convenience they had cooked up. They didn't wear rings. They didn't really talk to each other more than once every few years. He had no idea she had transferred to an engineering company, for example, or that she had volunteered to help with the fires. She probably had no idea he had gone to Africa. He didn't feel married, nor did he think of himself as a married man, except on paper.

In fact, he'd never thought of being married again. Not until Emma Selah suggested they should start seeing each other romantically. Suddenly, his situation with Martina loomed in the forefront of his mind. He should have told Emma at that exact moment, then explained who Martina was and what being married to her meant.

It was too late now.

Feeling less aggressive, calmer, he turned to leave the store. He stepped back into the parking lot and pulled up the funeral home's address on his phone. Martina's body had arrived that morning and would have been cremated by now. He needed to finalize the arrangements and see if the chaplain he'd contacted needed a ride from the airport.

Despite the home she'd made in Arizona, Martina wanted her ashes buried between her parents. He would see to that, then go to Arizona and meet with the company that handled renting out her house as a vacation home. He had to sign contracts and make sure any personal effects were removed from the home and put into her storage facility. All of the little details involved in closing up a life lived here on earth would take less than two weeks of his bereavement leave.

The unit filed into the briefing room. Emma followed, entering last, then stood against the back wall instead of joining the men in the seats. Through Colonel Jenkins speaking followed by Captain Norton, she tried not to look in

Jorge's direction, which was hard because he sat next to Norton.

He'd come back yesterday, and she'd managed to find a reason to be well away from the team's area. She couldn't avoid this briefing, though.

Then it became his turn to speak, to deliver the details of the mission brief. She'd checked the calendar this morning. She only had two months left of this contract. She couldn't wait to be done with it.

Embarrassment filled her heart as she thought about the many women she had watched fall into deployment affairs with married men over the years. She'd never understood why someone would do something like that. And here she was, a veteran of one of the things she abhorred most of all.

Did she own any accountability for that? She distinctly remembered asking him if he loved anyone back home and he'd said no. She'd fulfilled her end of the requirements.

Unable to look at him any longer, she glanced down at her boots. The worst part was that everyone knew. It was too small of a community to get away with having a secret love affair. Everyone had trod very carefully around her for the first week after Jorge left. She wanted to scream at them to quit, to go back to normal. But, nothing with this particular team could ever be normal again.

After Jorge sat down, Captain Norton took over the podium again and gave the last of the details regarding the CIA's request for the team's presence, including Emma, in an outpost about two hundred kilometers away. "If there are no other questions, we roll out of here in two hours." As everyone stood, he looked at her. "Selah, a word."

Her muscles tensed when Jorge stayed back with the captain. She decided she'd have to talk with him at some point, so it might as well be now.

She approached the front of the room and kept her eyes on Captain Norton. He lifted an eyebrow and asked, "Do you have the intel from the CIA, or do you need it?"

She held up the manila envelope in her hand. "I probably got a similar package to yours."

"Good." He gestured at Jorge. "Get with Peña and develop an interrogation strategy on this asset. I'd like us to get in and out of there."

"Yes, sir," she said, her throat tight around the words. As soon as the captain was out of earshot, she raised her head and asked, "Where would you like to work?"

He gestured at the seats around the room. "Here is good."

She pulled a chair out of a line and turned it around to face the other chairs. Sitting down, she opened the envelope and pulled out the brief folder. "I know of the group Al-Shabaab but not," she paused and looked at the name. "Moosa Habib. Isn't that group out of Yemen?"

He didn't answer her. Finally, she raised her eyes from the paper and caught him staring at her with a serious expression. "I'd like to explain."

Emma pressed her lips together and carefully worded her reply. "You had three months to explain. If I wanted to get technical, there's been two full years. I'd like to be fully briefed on this mission. Let's just stay on task."

"There has been a lot of time. And all that time—and everything—but you won't even hear me out?"

"Were you really married? You actually had a wife this whole time? You went home to bury your wife?"

"Yes, but..."

"No. No buts." She held up a hand in a halting motion. "I know everything I need to know. Anything else you have to say won't make a difference. Let's just get back to work."

He searched her face, and she kept her expression stoic. Finally, he sighed an exasperated sigh and said, "They are in Yemen. Moosa Habib is trying to develop a sect here in Djibouti. The CIA captured him infiltrating an outpost. So far, they have been unsuccessful in getting any good information out of him. We're the closest team to their location. They have asked for our expertise."

"I'm sure it was hard for them to admit it." She looked back down at the paper. "They've had him for three days?"

"Yes."

She thought about some of the tactics that might have been used on him until now. "Has he slept?"

"No."

She nodded. "Good. It will give us a bargaining chip." She tapped her lip with the side of her finger. "I'll go study up on Mr. Habib. I'll see you at the rally point in two hours."

As she started from the briefing room, he said, "She was only a friend. A fellow survivor of the greater Los Angeles foster care system. We got married for legal reasons."

She paused. What did legal reasons mean? Then she turned and faced him. "Nevertheless. Married."

Sorrow etched deep lines into his face. His brown eyes held little light. "I've been kicking myself for weeks now." His voice sounded weak, tired. "I've replayed every conversation we had a hundred times, and I can tell you where I went wrong."

She stared at him for several seconds, then said, "So can I. See you at the rally point." She didn't look in his direction again.

Some major part of her wanted to make him feel better, and she didn't like that. She didn't approve of that part of herself. She didn't need to make him feel better for lying to her and withholding important information that embarrassed her.

Her words replayed in her mind. "Are you in love with someone back home or something? Got a girl at Bragg?"

"No." He had answered. Not lying, technically. If only she had asked if he were married. No. If only he had not omitted that rather important fact.

Instead of going back to her quarters, she went to the headquarters building and requested the use of an empty conference room. That allowed her to spread the reports on the table and helped her build a profile of Mr. Moosa Habib.

She opened her notebook and started creating a diagram and a plan of action on how to get under his skin, get him to talk to her. By the time the alarm on her watch went off, she'd just finished gathering all of the papers back up and felt ready to face the prisoner.

As she mentally concluded her plan of action and tucked it away, her mind immediately brought Jorge back to the front of her awareness. When would she stop thinking about him all the time? How much longer would she have to suffer like this?

She went back to her containerized housing unit, her CHU. Laying the folder open on her cot, she spread the papers out and read while she changed clothes. She put on the standard Army uniform stripped of any badges, patches, or nametapes. She changed her comfortable brown suede leather boots for sturdy black leather boots with steel toes. Inside her right boot, she put a knife holster and slipped her six-inch steel commando knife into it. She bent and twisted and made sure it didn't hinder her movements.

After taping a page filled with Moosa Habib's background information to the mirror, she slowly braided her hair, memorizing the facts on the paper. As she secured the band to the end of her braid, she closed her eyes and dictated the names of the people in his family, his educational background, and his financial status. She double-checked her memory, then checked the time. She had about ten minutes to get to the rally point.

She packed the file into her bag, slipped a ballistic vest with added ceramic plates over her head, and found her canteen in her foot locker. She poured bottled water into it, grabbed her backpack, and rushed out of the building.

Thankfully, her quarters weren't too far from the rally

point. When she arrived, she realized she was the last one there. Captain Norton looked her up and down. "Hey. We were about to start without you. Ready?"

She knew he meant more than just physically. In reply, she nodded and added, "Affirmative. I know him better than his mama does."

"Good." As Emma started for the closest Land Cruiser, Norton put his hand on her elbow. "Quick word, Selah." He led her away from the vehicles and the team. "Talk to me about Peña."

She stared into his green eyes, searching for what he wanted her to say. "He's from L.A. Abandoned by first his mother then grandmother. Grew up in the foster system. Kind of closed off and emotionally unavailable."

Impatience flashed in his eyes, and she had to fight to keep from stepping backward from the look. In a harsh tone she'd never heard directed at her before, he said, "Without the sass, talk to me about *you* and Peña."

"Nothing to tell, sir," she replied. "He's married, right? Why would I involve myself with a married man?"

His beard moved as he clenched his teeth. "Emotions breed mistakes, Selah. You got your head in the game, or your heart?"

"Captain?" All innocence.

"You good to go twenty-four-ten?"

"Never better, Captain." She smiled to drive her point home. "You good?"

"Never better." He gestured with his head. "Load up in number two. I want you with Peña. You two need to work on your strategy. He'll be in the debriefing with you."

There was a time, rather recently in fact, that she would have relished a long drive through the desert sitting next to Jorge Peña talking shop. This was not that time. "Roger, sir. Wilco, sir."

The team loaded into the vehicles. Hanson drove the Toyota HiLux with Gill riding shotgun, Osbourne and Ibrahim in the back seat, and Chandler on the .50 caliber machine gun mounted in the bed. Ibrahim would quickly join him to help feed him ammunition if needed. The back window of the HiLux had been replaced with plastic.

In a Toyota Land Cruiser, Sanders got into the driver's seat, McBride took shotgun, and Norton and Morita climbed in the back.

That left one more Land Cruiser. Swanson took the driver's seat, Fisher took shotgun, and she and Jorge got into the back seat.

Hanson led the way, followed by Sanders, then Swanson. As the truck hit a rut and Emma's shoulder slammed into Jorge's, she thought it would be a long few hours of a ride.

CHAPTER
★

SEVEN

The Land Cruisers had been modified with the addition of thick armor plates and beefed-up suspension. While it afforded some protection from small-arms fire and IEDs, it also subtracted interior space. Add to that the thick body armor that everyone wore and their gear, and the space inside was, well, close.

Jorge made notes on his tablet as Emma walked through her profile of Moosa Habib. The entire hour they'd sat crammed together in the backseat, she hadn't looked him in the eye once. Every word out of her mouth was delivered in a pleasant, business-like tone. No hostility, but definitely no warmth.

Appreciative of the apparent truce, he focused on the mission. Right now, he couldn't afford the distraction. Even when it came at him like the faint smell of strawberries wafting from her hair.

Emma took her helmet off and pulled her ear bud out of her ear. "My radio quit working about ten minutes ago."

He frowned and said, "What about your mic?"

She turned her body away from him and pressed the button on her mic. "Radio check," she said. He could hear her voice but not through the radio.

When she turned back to him, he shook his head. "No joy." Jorge keyed his mic. "Six, this is Four. Be advised. Translator is down on comms. Over."

After a few seconds, Norton's voice came over the net. "Roger, Four. Probably the battery. Heat kills them quick. Plenty of spares in here with me. We'll fix it first break. Out."

Jorge looked at her and said, "Daddy says we'll swap out your batteries first time we stop."

"Hopefully, it won't matter," she nodded.

An hour into the journey, Captain Norton's voice came through the speaker in his helmet, ordering the convoy to stop. Immediately, Jorge turned his tablet off and shut the protective case. He glanced over at Emma, who obviously noticed the change in speed. "What is it?" she asked

"Unknown."

The terrain outside of the vehicles was brown and mountainous. The sun shone bright in the blue sky, offering not a single cloud. Before the vehicle stopped all the way, Jorge was out, his weapon ready. The surprisingly heavy armored door swung slowly shut behind him. Before he stepped forward, he heard Norton in his ear. "Bring Selah."

He pulled the heavy door back open and ducked his head into the vehicle. "Daddy wants you."

She didn't hesitate as she opened the door opposite him and got out of the vehicle. They walked up to the second vehicle just as Norton got out.

Fisher and Swanson moved to the front of the line of vehicles to watch for enemy movements. He knew Hanson and Brock took up the rear and behind him, Ibrahim joined Sanders on the .50-caliber machine gun and stood ready to feed the beast near the belted ammunition.

"Just got credible intel that Kamyar Punjabi is in a village about twenty clicks east of here."

Emma gasped. Jorge looked at her as the face of Kamyar Punjabi, the purported leader of Ansar ul-Ahar, came immediately to his mind. They'd located the nuclear bomb two years ago and prevented a devastating attack. However, the leader of the group had fled. He was number two on the most wanted list.

Emma looked at Jorge for the first time. "Has there been any chatter?"

He shook his head. "Not that I've seen or heard, but I've been gone for two weeks and Punjabi wasn't my focus when I got back."

"If Punjabi's here, something big is about to happen," Emma said.

Norton said, "Our new orders are to go and collect Punjabi and find out exactly that." He glanced up at the sky then back at Jorge. "What do you need to prep for a conversation with one Kamyar Punjabi?"

Jorge gestured behind him. "Everything I'd need is on my tablet."

Norton looked at Emma. "You?"

She pursed her lips. Jorge knew the extensive study she did before conducting any tactical debriefing with anyone. "I would have to see what Lieutenant Peña has with him. My files are not here."

"Understood." He glanced at his watch. "You have twelve minutes."

Without argument, Jorge and Emma turned and trotted back to their vehicle. He quickly accessed his file on Punjabi and handed the tablet to her. While she scanned and flipped pages, he studied her face, admiring the focus and concentration that drew her eyebrows together.

Her eyes moved rapidly. She clicked through page after page until she looked up. Without expression, she said, "I'm good except for comms."

Jorge nodded and turned slightly away from her as he pressed his mic button. "We're good, Six."

A second later, he received an acknowledgment, just as two Army UH-60 Blackhawk helicopters landed. The team loaded their weapons and ammunition into the helicopters.

Norton divided the team into two, and Jorge followed Emma into their assigned helicopter and sat next to her. Before she mounted her bird, Morita handed her a fresh battery for her radio.

"It's good. I tested it myself. Replace yours as soon as you stop moving for a minute."

The battery for the personal radio rig rested in the small of her back beneath her heavy body armor. She would have to sit somewhere that allowed for her to remove the body armor, remove the radio rig, swap the battery, re-attach the radio rig, then put her ballistic body armor back on. Not technically hard to accomplish, but it would take about five minutes and right now they had no time to spare before flying away and the helicopters were too crowded to afford her the space to accomplish the task.

She threw him a thumbs up and stowed the battery in the front cargo pocket of her ballistic vest.

Hanson, Sanders, Morita, Norton, Ibrahim, and Chandler got into one Blackhawk. Emma, Jorge, Gill, Osbourne, Fisher, McBride, and Swanson got into the other. The Blackhawks had not been rigged for personnel transport so the team assumed this flight was a hasty mission for them as well

They all took their helmets off and sat on them like little stools on the bare metal deck, a practice dating back to the Vietnam war which had saved the lives of many future families. The crew chief checked that the doors were secured then passed around headsets and they could all suddenly hear each other over the constant noise of the rotors and the two General Electric T700 turboshaft engines directly overhead.

While they flew, Jorge listened with one ear as Norton briefed the team while he studied different satellite images, trying to find evidence of heavily guarded buildings, unusual electronic signatures, or excessive power generation. He intercepted the communication from headquarters that explained which building positively housed Punjabi.

When Emma put her hand on his arm, he whipped his head in her direction, startled at the touch. "Sorry," she shouted off mic. "I said your name."

Without keying his mic, he pointed to his ear and yelled, "Chatter."

"Right. Sorry." She held her hands out, palms up. "I'm unarmed."

He didn't reply with words. Instead, he pulled his 9mm SIG Sauer M18 pistol from the holster he wore on his thigh. Holding the muzzle straight up and down the entire time, he removed the clip, pulled the slide back to make sure no round occupied the chamber, let the slide slam forward again, engaged the safety, replaced the clip, then flipped the gun like a pancake with one hand and held it out to her, pistol grip forward. The exercise took about four seconds. She accepted it without a word and held it in her left hand carefully keeping the muzzle pointed down and her finger out of the trigger housing.

"Need a knife?" he yelled.

She shook her head and gestured toward her boot.

Satisfied she didn't need anything else from him, he refocused on the conversation happening through the speaker.

"Pina Colada," Norton said over the net and unnecessarily leaned forward as if about to whisper. "What intel can you give us about Punjabi's preferred security?"

He swiped on the tablet until he got to the page with the satellite imagery. "He always has backup." He held out his tablet. "These satellite images of the village came in from AFRICOM twenty minutes ago. Looking at this, I'm thinking buildings A and C house added security. He's in what HQ has designated X."

Norton studied it, then nodded as he handed it back. "He's going to know we're coming."

"Without a doubt." Jorge pulled a map out of his breast pocket and folded it so the village was centered. "We started flying in his direction seven minutes ago. Let's give him five minutes for his people to realize we're on our way and get notification to him. Even if he starts to flee, there's nothing around. It's all wilderness for several kilometers around the village in every direction. That's assuming he has the technology to pick us up." He handed the map over. Norton looked at it and handed it back.

"Selah," Hanson asked, "Ever interrogated Punjabi?"

She shook her head. "I've researched him and his family. He's a bad dude. Full of hate and greed, and they drive each other. Everything he does he rationalizes with a platform of religious zealousness; however, his faith is a façade. He didn't enter a mosque until he was twenty-nine years old and about to bomb a girls' school in Iraq."

Hanson frowned. "Why is it always the girls' schools?" he muttered into the mic.

Norton addressed the whole team with the plan of attack. "Be ready. They may know we're coming," he added after laying out the plan. He looked at Emma. "Do you have any questions?"

"No, sir."

"Your comms still not working?"

"Not yet, sir. Have to open up the body armor to swap the battery out. Just need a few minutes."

"Right. Stick tight to Pina Colada. Like a shadow."

"Roger."

★ ★ ★

The helicopters set down in churning clouds of dust. They had swapped out their headsets for their combat helmets a few minutes earlier and the crew chief had opened the cargo doors. The instant one wheel touched the hard ground, Norton gave the hand signal to go. Emma found herself between Jorge and Hanson, pistol in hand. Her heart pounded with adrenaline, and the blood roared in her ears. Everything came into sharp focus. It felt like time slowed down.

As they moved further away from the helicopter, her military training kicked in. It had been several years since she'd been in the midst of combat. Since becoming a contractor, they always brought her in after the action settled down. She found a part of her surprised that Norton had her in the first wave. She had a feeling if he had gotten the news about Punjabi while they were on base, he would have sent for her once they secured the location.

The helicopters took off as soon as the team had fully exited to the ground. She watched the one on the other side of the village rise up and knew the other half of the team was on the ground over there. The helicopter pilots would take either end of the only road that went through the village and monitor for movement coming or going.

She stayed right beside Jorge. The team broke off here and there, clearing buildings and coming back together as a group. She could picture the village layout in her mind and knew they approached the buildings in the center of the village that intel claimed housed Punjabi and his men. As Osbourne and Fisher entered a building, a gunshot came from another.

Jorge ducked behind a stone wall. He glanced back at Emma. She wished he wouldn't think about her presence and just do his job. Worrying about her might cause him to make a mistake he wouldn't otherwise make.

She gave him a thumb's up. Concrete bits rained down on them as a bullet hit the wall above their heads. She ducked even further. McBride and Swanson rushed past her. McBride had his sniper rifle in a sling on his back. He knelt and fired his weapon as Swanson burst through the door of the building across the street. The two ran inside, rifles ready. The sound of a short burst of gunfire came from inside the building.

Emma's fingers itched to hold an automatic rifle or

carbine. Instead, she held the pistol ready. Everything she'd learned from combat came back to her and any hesitancy or fear floated away on the waves of her training.

She knew Jorge could hear the team in his helmet speaker. She didn't have that. She had to rely on him to give her direction. The noise of McBride's sniper rifle firing filled the square.

"We're going to that truck," Jorge said, rising in his crouch. "On my mark."

On three, they ran twenty feet down the road. Emma crouched next to the front tire. No one fired on them. They paused. Jorge motioned to a building with his hand. She nodded, and they ran into the doorway. A man swung out from behind a doorway, clutching a Kalashnikov rifle. Emma didn't even hesitate as she sited her pistol and fired two shots. Jorge rushed forward, checking the rest of the area beyond the doorway, shooting two bullets at a man who came out of a closet.

Once they checked and made sure both men no longer presented a threat, Emma took the opportunity to take the Kalashnikov from the man closest to her. She checked the magazine and peered through the iron site, testing the unfamiliar weight. She casually handed Jorge back his pistol. He chambered a round, re-engaged the safety, then holstered the weapon.

Horror at the idea of taking the life of another human being reared up and tried to take over her mind, to paralyze her while she processed the jumble of emotions trying to cloud her thoughts. She pushed it back, promising herself a quiet moment to unpack it as soon as they were back on American soil.

She sidled up next to Jorge as he knelt at the doorway. "Good?" he asked.

"Don't worry about me." She glanced through the doorway and then put her head back inside. "Just do your job."

He grinned and motioned to the truck parked in front of the building next to them. "Go."

They ran. Bullets peppered the ground in front of them. Emma slid and hid against the front tire, knowing the engine block would stop any bullet headed her way. The shooter didn't even waste any more ammunition on them.

Jorge said, "Roger," and looked over at her. "Confirmed sighting of Punjabi in that building over there." He pointed across the street.

"That's not building X," she remarked.

"It wasn't even in my initial estimation," he said. He raised his carbine and fired, then ducked back down. "I think it was an intentional cover."

"Likely. He's avoided capture this entire time. He's clever."

"Yeah. He's always the smartest fox in the henhouse, isn't he?"

Wow. She missed Jorge's clever wit and dialogue. Suddenly, though, she remembered why she hadn't spoken to him in a few weeks. The pain lanced her heart with a fresh wound. She felt the smile slide off her face, and she looked away from him, intentionally focusing back on the matter at hand.

Norton, Morita, and Sanders ran toward them then slid behind the truck for cover. Jorge took in their environment, made eye contact with Norton, and said, "Swap out your battery."

Emma felt very exposed but less so because the men around her stood watch. She was probably safer right now than back in her Dallas apartment. She retrieved the battery from the front cargo pocket of her vest then grounded it and leaned her rifle against the truck tire it to give it some protection from the dust. If Norton had an opinion about her possession of the weapon, he kept it to himself. Following her training, she grounded her helmet then removed her body armor and draped it atop the helmet as quietly as possible. The ceramic plates tended to thunk on the Kevlar combat helmet. She then began the process of swapping out the battery.

When she disconnected the spent battery and removed it from its casing, she quickly dropped it to the dirt. It felt so hot it almost burned her fingertips, like grabbing a hot frying pan handle. No wonder it hadn't worked. The men around her didn't see. Their attention was everywhere else, keeping her safe, so she took a second to blow on her fingertips before replacing the battery and putting the radio rig back together. That accomplished, she quickly reversed the process of donning her gear.

Once she stood back up fully reset, she keyed her mic twice. The three men around her clearly heard the clicks and visibly relaxed. She keyed her mic again. "We need him alive," she murmured.

"That's the plan," Jorge replied. His tone had cooled from before but they had other priorities at the moment. To Sanders, he asked, "How many are in there?"

"We've seen four different faces with the scopes. Intel from an hour ago counts seven bodies using thermal." Sanders pointedly looked between Jorge's holstered M18 and Emma's Kalashnikov. "Where'd you find that?"

She looked down at the weapon. "I took it."

When she met Sander's stare again, he narrowed his eyes at her, clearly studying her expression. "You okay?"

"Not the time or place, Drumstick," she said. "Let's keep working."

His grin was quick but superficial. His slow nod was more sincere. Then he turned to Jorge. At his signal then two men knelt and Norton drew in the dirt. "Jerry Maguire and Pot Pie are still on overwatch." He marked the two tallest buildings with X's. "We have MMMBop, Trout, Gilligan, and Commando taking building D on the west side of the village. We'll have Doc Oz and Honest Abe coming at this building from the rear. The rest of us will hit it from the front."

Jorge nodded as Norton keyed his mic and Morita relayed the orders to the rest of the team. "On my mark, gentlemen." He paused. "Try not to kill Punjabi. Pina Colada has a few questions for him. Wounded is fine, but we need him talking." He looked at Emma. "You stay here and monitor comms until we come back to get you."

She threw him a thumbs up. These men would operate

like a finely tuned engine, and she would act like a wrench in the works of that harmony if she were in their midst in the next few minutes.

As soon as he gave the go, the loud cracks of sniper fire filled the air. While McBride and Swanson covered them, they sped toward the building, weapons ready. Emma waited, looking at the door to the building over her rifle sites. The sound of men yelling filled the air.

The crack of a sniper rifle came from the other side of the building. Swanson must have stopped someone from leaving through that door. She saw no movement from her angle.

CHAPTER

★

EIGHT

With his gun trained toward the building, Jorge ran in the direction of the door. Sanders ran in front of him, Norton right behind. They reached the building and pressed their backs against the clay wall. When everyone acknowledged their positions, Norton gave the go and Sanders kicked in the door.

As Jorge went in low, he heard the crack of McBride's rifle but didn't turn to look in the direction of the shot. Instead, he yelled in Arabic for everyone to put their hands up. He counted five men. As he came all the way into the building, he realized he'd miscounted. A man sat cowering against the far corner, covering his face with his hands.

They gathered all of the men and searched them, removing weapons, phones, and various personal articles. When Wade brought the man from the corner forward, Jorge paused, studied his face. He recognized Punjabi, and communicated as much to Norton as he grabbed the man and turned him toward the wall, then pushed him against it. He spread his feet with his boots and searched him. He found no phone, no weapon. Then he turned him back around. For the slightest second, he caught the contempt in the man's eyes, before it was replaced with fear.

Jorge kept his gun trained on him. Most of the men they'd captured today were well groomed with trimmed beards and clean clothing. Jorge wondered if this was Punjabi in disguise or if his organization had leaked someone else's photo to throw off the western enemies. It honestly could go either way.

He knew Emma would likely know for sure. She'd studied his family extensively and would have seen photos of him throughout the phases of his life.

Sanders' voice came through his earpiece. "Clear!"

He glanced at the stairwell as Hanson marched another captured prisoner down the stairs, Sanders on his heels.

Norton approached, his eyes hard, his mouth in a tight line. Jorge knew he was hyper-focused right now and would stay this way until his entire team was out of danger. He gave a slight motion with his head, and Jorge nodded. "Honest Abe, can you take over?"

"Yes, sir," Ibrahim said, sidling up next to him and training his weapon toward Punjabi and the man next to him.

Jorge followed Norton into the now empty kitchen. They both stood where they could see both the doorway and the window and spoke in low tones.

"What do you think?" his captain asked.

Jorge ran the palm of his hand over his beard and adjusted the helmet on his head. "It's definitely who we know as Punjabi. But he's evaded capture this long for a reason."

"What would Selah know?"

Jorge glanced at the window. "Probably more than us."

Norton nodded. He pressed the button on the microphone. "MMMbop, get that single room structure next to us cleared. Make sure there are no hidden exits or weapons and we'll use it as a holding cell."

"Sir," Hanson affirmed.

Norton pulled a notepad out of one of the pockets on his vest. He used the stub of a pencil to write. He paused and hit the mic again. "Jerry Maguire, Pot Pie, report."

Jorge listened to the snipers affirm no activity. He said, "Sounds like they had the village to themselves."

"Yeah." He looked at his watch, noted the time on his notebook, and then slipped it back into the pocket. "Okay, let's get Selah in here. I want you two on the same page."

He'd give anything to be back on the same page as her. "Yes, sir."

He went back through the main room and out the front door, then trotted over to where he'd left Emma. Only, she wasn't there.

★ ★ ★

Emma crouched next to the truck's front wheel. The engine block and the wheels would act as both cover and concealment for the next few minutes. She listened silently as the team took the building. The last voice she had heard over her radio had been Jorge's, then her radio had gone dead again.

She realized that her radio rig itself must have a short. That would explain why her first battery had powered the rig for about ten minutes then stopped. It would also explain why that first battery had felt so hot to the touch when she swapped in the new one. Whatever was wrong with the hardware, it had obviously shorted this fresh battery out after a few minutes, too.

As frustrated as her downed radio made her feel, the majority of her frustration came from thoughts of Jorge whose voice still echoed in her ears. She could still feel that strong pull of attraction for the man and wondered what was wrong with her. Why had she let him get under her skin?

Who cares if he had an explanation about the mystery wife? It shouldn't matter what the explanation was. He had no business trying to kiss her while he was married to someone else.

So why did she still feel so drawn to him?

She sighed, leaned her rifle against the truck tire beside her, and pulled her tablet out of her pocket. She needed to quit thinking about Jorge. Instead, she focused on the file she had on Punjabi. She reviewed text and documents that she had read dozens of times, doing her utmost to keep every detail fresh in her mind. She flipped to his photograph and zoomed in.

Suddenly, she shut the tablet off. Even as she had stared into the black eyes of the terrorist, Jorge's face swam in front of her vision. She squeezed her eyes shut, mentally reprimanding herself for the distraction.

Then she felt the muzzle of a rifle against the side of her neck.

"Touch that gun and I kill you," a man said in accented English.

She'd set her weapon down and picked up her tablet – in the middle of a combat zone. This was her fault. It took a millisecond for Emma to consider all of her options. If this guy wanted her dead, she'd already be dead. The best conclusion was to do what this man said and trust Jorge and his team to rectify her lack of situational awareness as soon as possible.

She dropped the tablet beside her and kicked some sand over it as she rose to her feet, leaving her AK-47 where it rested against the truck tire slightly behind her. She held her hands up about shoulder height.

Her mouth had gone dry and she saw little specs dance in front of her eyes. Should she turn? Could she take on this man using the knife in her boot when he retrieved the weapon?

Then she heard a second voice and knew trying to fight off two men would be foolish.

"Check her for other weapons," the second man said in Arabic. "Then take her gun."

Emma closed her eyes and endured the search. He found her cell phone, but didn't find the knife. They didn't look for, or find, the tablet. When he finished the intrusive search, he spoke in English again. "Go. This way. Move."

Hands still up, wishing she had a working mic, she turned. One man walked toward a building about twenty feet away. He wore a pair of desert-camouflage pants that looked like Russian issue and an olive-green shirt that resembled Chinese military issue. He held a parachutist modified AK-47 with the stock folded and also had a TT-30 Tokarev pistol tucked into his belt.

The man training his rifle on her wore a white robe with a goldenrod vest. He had a black mustache and mean eyes. He gestured with his rifle to emphasize the directions, and Emma followed the first man, letting this one get behind her.

If she screamed, the team would hear her. These two men would be killed almost before the sound faded from the air. However, so would she. If she stayed alive, she might be able to glean some information that could prove helpful.

Keeping her head as still as possible, she looked all around, desperate for one of her team to come out of a building or look their direction from the sniper towers.

When she reached the doorway, she looked for a way to subtly mark the door but found nothing. The man behind her pushed her forward with the muzzle of his rifle, the hard metal digging into her back.

When her eyes adjusted to the dim interior, she investigated the room. A single bed sat against the far wall. Under the window sat a porcelain wash basin on a small table. In the center of the room lay a red and green rug.

The first man bent and pulled on the corner of the rug. It actually served as the handle to a trap door. He didn't even glance their way as he walked down the steps and disappeared. The man behind her shoved her forward with the gun's barrel. "Go. You go."

Heart pounding, the copper taste of fear flooding her mouth, she slowly walked, praying the entire time that they were seen, that the team was being dispatched right now. However, no one burst through the door to rescue her. Instead, she slowly climbed down the steps and into the basement of the building.

CHAPTER
★
NINE

He'd thought his adrenaline ran high until it kicked into high gear at the sight of her tablet on the ground, sand skittering over the screen. Jorge looked all around but saw no movement. He muted the radio chatter and listened, but heard nothing but the whisper of the breeze.

Forcing himself to stop panicking, he turned the radio back on and keyed his mic. "Hey, MMMbop, is Selah assisting you?"

A second later, Hanson gave a negative reply. He

scooped her tablet up off the ground and said, "Daddy, a moment, please."

"Meet me in building X," Norton said.

Mindful of possible snipers waiting for them to lower their guard, Jorge strategically moved from cover position to cover position and worked his way to the building in the center of the village. When he went through the doorway, weapon ready, he spotted Norton and Sanders.

"Selah's missing," Jorge said. He held up her tablet. "This was on the ground."

Emotion flared in Norton's eyes as he accessed his mic. "McBride, see any movement on your six recently?"

"No, sir."

Sanders looked out the window. "How?"

"It would only take one person. Our focus was securing that building."

Jorge clenched his teeth. "I should have kept her with me."

"Against regulation, you mean?" Norton shook his head. "I should have left someone with her." He spoke into the mic again. "Pale horse, this is sand spur. Over."

The Blackhawk squadron commander responded instantly. "Sand spur, this is pale horse. Go ahead, over."

"Pale horse, be advised adversaries have taken our translator hostage. We are preparing for a PR. Can you report on any unusual activities or movement at your locations, over?"

The warrant officer in the other helicopter reported, "This is pale horse west. That's a negative. No movement.

Over."

The Blackhawk squadron commander concluded, "Pale horse east. Negative here. All clear, sand spur. Nobody in or out. We would have seen them from our vantage point. Over."

"Roger, pale horse. Please stand by for now. Over."

After a few seconds, the Blackhawk squadron commander replied, "Roger, sand spur. Standing by and will support your PR any way we can. Over."

Norton said, "Roger, out." Then to Sanders on the team net he said, "Haven't left the village."

Sanders scrubbed at his black beard. "Then they're here."

Jorge watched Norton's face as he analyzed and processed. Finally, he nodded. "Bring me Punjabi."

★ ★ ★

Where the upstairs was sparse and primitive, this room had a bank of monitors on one wall and three laptops on a long table. Steam rose from an electric kettle and a soccer game silently played out on a small color television. The man who had opened the hidden door spoke in low tones to an older man with a white beard. The man studied her as she stopped in the center of the room.

"*Ma asmuk?*" the white-haired man asked in Arabic. What is your name? Emma chose not to give away the fact that she spoke his language fluently.

She shook her head. "I don't understand," she said in English.

The man raised an eyebrow and ran his gaze from the top of her black hair to the toes of her black steel toed boots. "Where you come from?" he asked in English.

"Texas." After a second, she added, "United States."

He shook his head. "No. Where your people from? You are not *kawaja*." Unsurprisingly, he used the pejorative term for "white people" common to northern Africa and parts of the Kingdom of Saudi Arabia.

She had a ready cover story. "Türkiye." She rapidly spoke in Turkic, a language not remotely related to Arabic. "Do you speak Turkic?"

"Not good," he replied and continued in English. "Why your soldiers invade my village?"

She glanced quickly at the screens on the wall. Only one was on, showing a camera view of the street outside of the building. "We are here to question Kamyar Punjabi."

He waved his hand as if dismissing her. "Punjabi! Bah! Punjabi not come here. This is a peaceful village."

She bit her tongue in retort of asking where the women and children of this "peaceful" village were. Instead, she said, "If what you say is true, if Punjabi's not here, then we won't stay long."

Without warning, he slapped her across the face with the boney back of his leathery hand. The sting immediately brought tears to her eyes. She ducked her head and blinked, trying to overrule her body's natural reaction. "You do not speak to me unless I ask you a question."

Hands grabbed her from behind and forced her roughly into a chair. They did not bother, however, to tie her hands or feet. They had assessed her as a weak woman who posed no threat just as she hoped. If she needed to, she could retrieve the knife from her boot.

A radio in the guard's hand crackled. The older man took it from him and walked over to the furthest corner of the room, speaking too quietly for Emma to overhear him. When he returned, he said, "The men know you're gone. They search for you. I don't think they find you here. What they exchange for you?"

She raised an eyebrow. "If you're suggesting exchanging me for Punjabi, they won't. I'm not as important as he is."

"You no good for trade?" He asked. "Maybe I sell you to Greek man I know who likes women from Türkiye."

Not willing to take his bait and reply, she kept her head lowered. *Please, God,* she thought, *bring Jorge.*

CHAPTER

★

TEN

The wind had picked up. Jorge stood outside a small adobe building and took a drink out of his canteen, then surveyed the area. The air had a feel to it he'd experienced before, and he hoped he was wrong. The last thing they needed weas a sand storm.

Worry clawed at the back of his mind, trying to take over his thoughts and remove his caution. They'd searched the entire village. She'd been missing for at least twenty minutes.

"There has to be something we're not seeing," Ibrahim said, tightening the lid on his own canteen. "A hidden cache."

He glanced at the building that housed Captain Norton. He had Punjabi in there, but the man pleaded and cried like a woman, babbling in Arabic too fast for Jorge to understand, insisting his name was Omar. Jorge had caught the look in his eye before his act began, and knew he was lying.

Ibrahim had questioned him at length, but he'd not changed his story. He looked up at the sky. "When will the Hawkeye be in range?"

The US Navy's favored E-2 Hawkeye is a twin engine, five crewmember, high-wing turboprop aircraft with a 24-foot diameter radar rotodome attached to the upper fuselage. It can coordinate all kinds of signals from land, sea, air, and space. It's an all-weather, carrier-based tactical battle management airborne early warning, command and control aircraft that AFRICOM had hastily tasked to support this mission. They would utilize it to get heat readings from the buildings.

"Seven minutes."

As he started to look back down, the sun hit something on the corner of the roof across from him. He frowned and stepped closer. A webcam. He had personally searched the building. It didn't even have a sink, much less an electrical outlet. How did it support a webcam?

Instead of continuing forward, he turned and accessed his mic. "Hey, Daddy," he said, "I spy with my little eye a security camera."

"Standby."

Seconds later, Captain Norton trotted toward him. Jorge blocked the camera with his body and gestured with his hand. "My four. We cleared it. There's nothing in that building."

"Mayhap there is and mayhap there ain't. One of the huts had a hidden basement. I have Ozzy and MMMBop going back through each one, checking for access." He glanced at Abe. "I need you with the prisoner, Sergeant. You're the only one besides Emma who can communicate with him. Doc Oz can back you up." Captain Norton looked everywhere but at the camera. "We have recon photos coming in six minutes. We'll be able to tell if there are bodies below that building."

"Unless they're blocking it somehow."

Norton sighed. "I know you want to storm it, but wisdom says we wait."

"Every second she's in there –"

"You don't know for a fact she is. If there's only a single access point to a hidey-hole, they could kill her before we get to her. Best we can do right now is to wait and gather as much intel as possible."

Jorge took a breath and tried to project a calm he didn't feel. "Wasn't it Patton who said, 'A good plan violently executed now is better than a perfect plan executed next week.'? Right now, I'm all about some violent immediate executing."

Norton caught his eye. "Me too, and I'm not talking

about next week. Here's the plan. Intel first, then we immediately execute exactly enough violence."

Under different circumstances, he would advise Norton exactly in that manner. Except that Emma was the one somewhere with these terrorists. "Yes, sir," he said. "But if intel doesn't give us much, I'm still going in to check."

"I think you mean *we're* still going in to check."

The person who had deployed the webcam hadn't bothered to change the password from the factory default. It took Fisher less than three minutes to intercept the feed from the webcam and start transmitting a looped video. In that time, Captain Norton received word that the naval E-2 Hawkeye was in range and ready to transmit. Hanson sent the exact coordinates of the building in question. Within forty seconds, they received confirmation that they had readings of four adults in the subterranean area of the building.

Norton looked at his screen as Jorge peered over his shoulder. "Three men. This has to be Selah. Smaller frame."

Petite. Vulnerable. Jorge closed his eyes and shook his head. He had to get those thoughts out of his mind. One thing Emma Selah was not was vulnerable. She was actually highly trained and quite strong.

"Suggestions?" Norton asked.

Sanders looked at the small, square building. "It's one room. I'm going to guess floor access to a basement area.

The second our boots touch the floor, they'll hear us, know we're there."

"Agreed," Norton said. "So that's a problem. We need a solution."

"Rappel down from the roof?" Chandler asked.

Sanders looked up at the top of the building. "No way we could break through the roof without a whole mess of racket. Then we'd be too far away to do anything quickly."

Jorge agreed. "We'll just have to step lightly and move with as much alacrity as possible."

"Yes," Chandler said. "I say we prime grenades before infil. Get inside, open the hatch. Toss in flash bangs and gas. They'll be immobilized long enough for us to get down the hatch."

"Selah will be gassed along with them," Jorge said, remembering suffering through the gas chamber in basic training.

"She'll understand it and she'll live." Norton looked up at the sky. "Mr. Myagi, tell the flyboys and airborne sailors we need constant monitoring if they can spare the task time. Most ricky-tick. We don't want to keep her down there any longer than necessary. Commando, Drumstick, Pina Colada, you three take the lead. Move swiftly and silently. Let's surprise them." He turned and surveyed the village. "Gill and MMMBop, I want every hut's floor searched again. See if we missed any hatches or hidey holes. I don't want them going through some tunnel system and escaping."

Nerves began to dance in Jorge's gut. He didn't fight

them; he channeled them, bringing his mind into sharper focus. He conferred with Sanders and Chandler deciding the order of battle and things like who would carry live grenades and who would open the hatch.

Jorge slung his weapon and accepted two flash bangs and three gas grenades. Except for their markings, they looked like nearly identical cylinders. The flash bangs were smaller in diameter and the gas grenades were just about the size of a soda can. He prepared each of them first by pinching the cotter pins on the end of the pull rings together and then by carefully pulling the pins almost all the way out of the spoons. The slightest tug on the pins would pull them all the way out all at once. He ran a length of parachute cord through the rings, tied it in a loose noose, and left enough slack that he could pull the rings by tying the end off on his body armor and jerking his hands down rapidly.

He held all of them with his fingers and thumbs in a little pyramid of five cylinders with the gas grenades along his thumbs and the flashbangs beneath his fingers. He positioned them so that the spoons could fly free from his fingertips. Before they walked into the building, He would pull all five pins. Once they stepped inside and identified the hatch, Jorge would let all five spoons fly. Then, on the count of three-Mississippi, he would toss all five down the hole, after which things would get exciting.

That three seconds was critical. The grenades were supposed to have a five second fuse. They didn't want to give the enemy below five entire seconds to react.

However, a short fuse could result in a flashbang detonating early, in which case Jorge would need someone to shave for him for the rest of his life, assuming he lived.

When he had everything prepped, he threw them a thumbs up and carried his grenades up to them. Fisher confirmed that the feed remained captured. They could get to the door of the building without being seen, but once they crossed the threshold, they'd have to move swiftly. After putting on their gas masks, Sanders kindly tied off the loose parachute cord onto Jorge's shoulder strap.

Jorge led the way. At the door, Sanders sloshed cleaner, lubricant, and preservative, or CLP, from his weapons cleaning kit onto the door hinges and door handle. Chandler gave the countdown by folding fingers of his gloved hand into a fist, then Sanders opened the door, which swung silently on the newly greased hinges. Inside the hut, he saw the rug in the center of the floor. One corner was slightly rolled upward. He guessed that was the access. Jorge jerked down quickly, pulling all five grenade pins easily and silently.

Motioning with his hand, Sanders and Chandler moved forward, stepping as lightly as possible, rolling their steps from heel to ball of foot. Sanders kept his strong hand in control of his weapon and grabbed the corner of the rug with his weak hand and gave it a slight tug. It offered some resistance. This was more than the point of access; it was actually like the door handle. He made eye contact with each man, motioning for them to prepare to breach.

Jorge held the grenades over the rug and opened the tips of his fingers and thumbs. The five spoons fell soundlessly to the rug.

One-Mississippi.

Two-Mississippi.

On three-Mississippi, Sanders pulled hard on the rug, and the hatch opened enough for Jorge to toss in all five grenades.

The surprised voices of men became muffled as Sanders slammed the hatch shut. The three of them immediately donned their protective masks and cleared them seconds before they heard the explosions. As soon as the second explosion rang out, Sanders threw the hatch back open, and they went down the stairs, weapons ready. Jorge leaped in first, his deadly M-4 carbine pointing up and away from Emma's assumed position.

CHAPTER

★

ELEVEN

The men in the room did not look at her again. It gave Emma a chance to observe, store information in her mind, try to plan her escape. At one point, she watched the screen as the men of the unit conferred with one another. She'd seen Jorge look directly at the camera. Not long after, everyone left camera range. Since then, she'd seen no movement, not even shadows, from the team. That told her that someone, Fisher most likely, had hacked the stream and looped a video feed.

Would her captors realize?

They spoke Arabic in low tones. She caught enough of an occasional word to piece together that they planned to exchange her for Punjabi. However, she knew her team would not compromise the entire mission for her. They'd try to rescue her, of course. They would not, however, trade her in exchange for a high-profile prisoner. And she wouldn't expect them to.

The creak of a floorboard overhead made the men in the room go silent. All of them looked up at the monitor. Seeing no activity near the door, they continued talking.

Emma slipped her hand into her pocket and gripped her handkerchief in her fist. She guessed what would happen next and wanted to be as prepared as possible. Not that anyone could truly prepare for a gas attack.

She clandestinely stared up at the high-profile hatch in the ceiling. The second it creaked open, she turned her body away and pulled the handkerchief out of her pocket. The high-pitched metallic sound as the first canister hit the floor startled the men with her. They shouted as the remaining grenades landed, but it was too late. The hatch shut and concussive explosions, light, and gas filled the room. Emma knelt low.

On the ground, she pulled her knife out of its boot sheath and covered her nose and mouth with a handkerchief. Even so, her eyes started watering, her exposed skin burned, and the back of her throat began to feel raw. She gagged against the handkerchief. One of her captors ran past her, stumbling. She lashed out with her knife, stabbing him in the calf. He howled in pain and dropped his weapon as he grabbed her wrist with his hand. But the gas overwhelmed him and he almost immediately let her go, falling to the ground, gasping for air. Emma retrieved his rifle.

Three masked figures came through the hatch in the floor. Emma recognized Jorge immediately. He searched the room and she could tell when he finally saw her. The other two with him secured the rest of her captors as Jorge made his way to her. He knelt on the ground and held out a protective mask.

Once she had donned and cleared the mask, her eyes and sinuses still burned in a way that almost consumed her. She stumbled to her feet and retrieved her knife from the calf of the man, then helped Jorge secure his wrists. Once his hands were zip-tied behind his back, they marched him toward the stairs.

Captain Norton stuck his head through the hatch. When she got close to them, she recognized Sanders and Chandler as the men who had helped rescue her. Sanders guided his prisoner up the steep stairs, then Captain Norton retrieved him. Sanders helped Chandler get his prisoner onto the ladder. Jorge guided the wounded man up the ladder until Norton could get a hold of him.

Emma took off her gas mask in the hut and resisted the urge to press her forearm against her eyes. Her clothes were inundated with CS gas. She bent over and coughed and gagged. A canteen appeared in front of her face. She looked up to see Jorge holding his out to her. She took it from him, tilted her head back and splashed her face, letting the water run away from her open eyes, then took a long pull.

"Gonna make it?"

She put her hands on her hips and kept her eyes closed as she kept her face pointed toward the ceiling. "Better than I would if you hadn't come."

"True."

"I might vomit, though."

"Also true." He took his canteen back. "You took in a lot of the cyanocarbon known as 2-chlorobenzalmalononitrile. Bound to upset your tummy."

"You and your big words."

"Cyanocarbon?" he asked all innocence.

Emma shook her head. "Tummy." She tested her eyes. The burn was still there, but it was manageable now. The skin around them felt swollen and raw. "Got wet wipes?"

"Yeah," Jorge answered and held out the open package. "It's kind of hard to take you seriously when you're all red faced and puffy and crying and snotty like that."

"Ha ha." She pressed a wet wipe against her eyes and wiped away the excess tears and water. "They were wanting to trade me for Punjabi."

"I don't see that working out well."

"There was no plan. I was just an opportunity." Norton approached. When she made eye contact with him, embarrassed heat flooded her face. "Sir, I am —"

He shook his head. "I don't need to hear it."

She was distracted and she broke discipline in the

middle of a combat operation. He knew it and she knew it. But the bad comms was on him. They both knew that, too. Verbalizing all of that wasn't going to do anything good for anyone. "Yes, sir."

"Did you get anything down there?"

She shook her head. "There may be something on the computers, but I never actually could hear most of what they said. They stayed well away from me and talked very quietly. I tried to play it off like I didn't understand Arabic by speaking Turkic, but I don't think they bought it."

He nodded. "They haven't gotten this far for this long without being a little bit careful. I'm glad you're okay, Selah."

"Thank you, sir."

"All y'all need to get out of those clothes. You're making me want to go to MOPP-4 just standing here. Leave your radio with MMMbop so he can figure out why it died on you."

Norton walked away, leaving her alone in the corner with Jorge. He asked, "You want to talk about it?"

She clenched her teeth together and slipped her hands into her pocket so that she could squeeze them into fists without him seeing. "Nothing to talk about."

"You keep saying that, but there is an abundance to talk about."

"Like what? Secrets, lies? I thought I could work with you. I thought I could set you aside from the equation and still get my job done, but I don't think I can. I put myself and the team in danger because I was so distracted by you.

When we get back to base, I'll contact my company and have them send a replacement."

As she started to walk away, he said, "Emma."

She paused walking, but she did not turn around.

"I realized at some point during my trip back to the States that between the Gulf of Aden, a little tea shop on the River Walk, and all of these war-torn places in the corners of the world where we find our paths constantly cross, I managed to fall in love with you. I don't see that changing for the rest of my life."

A hundred responses ran through her mind. Her heart leaped at the idea of Jorge loving her. She had to remember the pain he caused her—the physical pain she felt when she found out about his wife. She did not reply. Instead, she walked through the building and out the door.

Jorge muttered, "*Obstinada!*" Stubborn.

★ ★ ★

They had stowed all their clothes in waterproof bags and washed off their boots and other essential gear as best they could. Fortunately, she had brought an entire spare uniform minus the boots and gear. The faint salty trace of CS that had gotten on their gear and skin still lingered around them like a halo, but that would go away after a long bath and a good dry cleaning. Emma's swollen face and bloodshot eyes had calmed down quite a bit and she had swallowed enough water that her voice didn't come out like a croak anymore.

Morita knocked on the door frame of the building.

"Birds have been recalled. Bad sand storm inbound. We're ordered to shelter in place and they'll return when it's clear. Hawkeye is still in orbit but they are asking permission to retask, too."

Emma's stomach knotted. She just wanted to get away from here.

Norton nodded and looked out the window. "We'll keep everyone together. Consolidate all prisoners in building Y. Keep them in the smaller back room packed in tight. Search everyone again so that we get no surprises during the storm. I want two man shifts with eyes on them the entire time. Gilligan and Drumstick, go back up Pot Pie and Jerry Maguire in their towers. Two by two."

"Yes, sir."

Emma stayed after everyone else left to see to Norton's orders. He approached her, his eyes serious. "Get your head right?"

"Not to my standards, but it will do." When she blinked, she could feel the swelling in her eyelids. "I'm gone as soon as we get back. You don't need to worry about me anymore."

He narrowed his eyes. "Gone?"

"Yeah. I thought I could ignore him, but I can't."

Norton rubbed impatiently at his beard and started to leave the room but turned back and said, "Listen up, Selah. It's a mistake, not hearing him out."

"So you've made clear." Angry tears filled her eyes, but she blinked them back. "Anything else, *sir*?"

A muscle ticked in his jaw. Annoyed, he said, "Matter

of fact there is. Get over to the building across the way. Fisher has the laptops from the basement, but we need help reading some of the data."

Finally, something that fell under her job scope. "Yes, sir."

As she started from the room, he stopped her. "Prisoners in there. Might want to cover up."

She glanced over her shoulder at him, nodded, then pulled a black silk scarf out of her pocket. Even though she'd already been seen by the men who took her captive, she thought it best to go ahead and cover up. It took seconds to secure the scarf around her head and fasten the end so that the bottom half of her face was covered. Usually, she'd put on black eyeliner, but the skin was too raw from the gas. This time she'd forgo that part of her disguise.

Outside, she looked on the horizon and saw the wall of sand heading their way. It looked like a giant brown tsunami crashing down on them. For a moment, her steps faltered. She'd seen some sand storms in her time, but this one probably rivaled most of them.

She brushed by Chandler, who stood guard at the door. Osbourne and Ibrahim stood guard at the doorway to the second room guarding the prisoners.

In the main room, Fisher sat in front of three open laptops. He looked up at her when she approached him. He stood and offered her the seat. They spoke quietly so the prisoners wouldn't hear. "I wanted to see if there was anything we could use against Punjabi. But once I broke the encryption, it's all in Arabic."

She took his seat and looked at the first laptop. It took a second for her brain to shift to reading Arabic, to move her eyes from right to left instead of left to right. It had been several months since she'd done so. "Do you know what we're looking for?" she asked, clicking open a document.

"Correspondence that would give us an idea of what they're planning," he said. "Perhaps mission plans or checklist with the entire mission mapped out in chronological order with names, addresses, and phone numbers." When she glanced up at him, he winked. "Kidding. Anything. You're the one who will speak with him. Use what you can."

Hanson brought two chairs in just as the first specks of sand peppered the glass window. The sand here was not like the sand in the Persian countries. There it was like a fine powder. Here it was grittier somehow. Emma glanced up and said, "It's here."

The door flew open and Hanson and Jorge came in, escorting Punjabi between them. Emma's heart increased speed, and she licked her lips. She wasn't ready to speak to him, and he definitely wasn't ready to speak to her. If they could hold him for a few days, deny him sleep, execute some simple deprivation and sensory tactics on him, they might wear him down enough to give her something to go on. But to speak with him, here in his element, she might as well be prepping to talk to a wall.

While Hanson sat him in the chair, the door opened and Norton blew in along with a cloud of sand, followed closely by Morita. He shut the door behind them and shook sand out of his hair like a dog shakes water off its back. The room grew dark as the windows rattled.

Emma glanced up at him as he approached her, then she turned her back to Punjabi and spoke very quietly. "What do you want to know?"

"His plans would be lovely," Norton said under his breath. "For now, just get started with a dialogue. We can continue back at the base once the storm clears."

She gestured at the laptops. "There are chemical components on here. I'm not a chemist, but I could write down the English if you have someone who could read them."

He tapped his ear. "Comms are down until the storm blows over. We'll work on it when we can." He put his hand on the back of her chair. "You are the one who can do this. You are the one who knows him. Don't be intimidated by anything here. You have the upper hand."

Hanson, Osbourne, Ibrahim, and Chandler went fully into the room with the prisoners and shut the door. She knew that was to keep them from overhearing her conversation with Punjabi.

She stood and crossed over to the chair across from Punjabi. Immediately, Jorge took up the sentry spot at her right shoulder. She appreciated his presence there more than he'd know.

The man across from her had his hands over his eyes and rocked back and forth. She could barely hear his mumbles over the storm. It wasn't an unusual tactic for the leader to pretend to be someone with a low status in the event of capture, but it was annoying. It took time she didn't appreciate wasting to break through the facade and have a conversation with the real person.

"It's good to meet you in person, Kamyar Punjabi. I just missed you a few years ago. You may call me Selah." The rocking motion continued, but the mumbling stopped. She said in Arabic, "Haafiz Durrani gave up your bomb in eleven minutes." He lowered his hands and glared at her. The meek, scared servant look vanished in the wake of fury. She'd smile, but he'd see it in her eyes, so she kept her face under the scarf expressionless. "Interested in how I did that?"

He looked her up and down. "How *you* did that? I don't believe you."

She gave a cocky shrug of her shoulder and settled back further in her chair. "You can ask him when you get to your eternal reward. He killed himself two days later. Or so they say. I think your people got to him."

"More likely your people got to him."

"Maybe. Still, I'd be careful if I were you. These men here lost loved ones in that cafeteria bombing last year. Now that you've finally admitted your identity, you're trapped in here with some pretty angry men."

He looked over her shoulder at Jorge and back to her. "I guess I should be glad you have rules."

She looked around. "I don't know. Storm's wiped out communication. It's just us. My story will be whatever they say it will be. You won't be alive to argue it. The only real question is this. Fast and painless or slow and painful?" She made eye contact with him again. "I'm sure you can understand."

Their back and forth continued. She could tell her knowledge of his life and the people in his life surprised him. Whenever he thought he had the upper hand, she took it from him. Soon he quit speaking altogether.

Finally, she stood. "Keep him separated from the other men. Don't give anyone a chance to silence him."

CHAPTER

★

TWELVE

Jorge stood over Emma's right shoulder, watching Punjabi. The man was weak. Maybe he was a good leader. Maybe he could inspire men to do terrible things. But he had a weak mouth, scared eyes, and was clearly out of his element surrounded by Jorge's team.

Emma came at him for an hour, relentlessly on the offense until he just quit responding and stared at the floor. Jorge had zero respect for him.

Finally, she said, "Keep him separated from the other

men," as she stood. The movement of her body caught his eye. Her small frame was such a dichotomy to the way she commanded a tactical debriefing. He thought he could spend the rest of his life watching her work. "Don't give anyone a chance to silence him."

Unfortunately, he wasn't there to watch her work. He was there to watch the prisoner. By taking his eyes off Punjabi for a heartbeat, he missed the subtle clues of his planned movement.

Before he could fully react, Punjabi lunged forward and pulled the knife out of Emma's boot. With wild eyes and a feral growl, he raised it above his head and brought it down just as Jorge stepped in front of her. The knife came down between his body armor and his collarbone and inserted itself neatly into his chest cavity. Jorge fired a three-round burst from his carbine, and both men went down.

Everything slowed down for a moment. Jorge was completely aware of the knife but felt nothing. The room filled with the yells and calls of the men in the holding room. Jorge turned his head as Sanders dragged Punjabi's body away, leaving a smeared blood trail in its wake.

Suddenly, Emma was there. She'd pulled the scarf off her head and pressed it all around the knife handle sticking out of him. The fear in her eyes made him want to soothe her, comfort her, but he couldn't find any words. Instead, he just looked at her, letting the beauty of her face consume all of his vision.

He held a hand up to brush her cheek, but she took it in both of hers. Wanting to let her know he was okay, he squeezed her hand.

Osbourne appeared. The medic was a medical doctor—Jorge had read his file—an oral surgeon from Miami who had joined the military after walking away from his residency.

Osbourne inspected the knife area. "Never anything simple with you, Pina Colada."

He thought simple was boring. But, again, no words would come out. It fascinated him how detached his brain became from his body.

"Status, Ozzy," Norton said, standing over them.

Osbourne looked at Emma first. Jorge could read the concern in his eyes. Then he looked up at Norton. "A transport bird two minutes ago would make me happy." Norton didn't give a response. After a beat, Osbourne said, "I can assume his lung is compromised. Without imagery, I have no way of knowing how close to the heart this is. It appears to be throbbing with every one of his heartbeats so I can guess but I don't know a definitive." He paused. "Other than very serious."

Emma licked her lips and put her hand on Jorge's forehead. Her hand was cool, soft. He closed his eyes and just relished the feel of her. Soon, their voices became buzzing sounds, and even though he tried very hard to keep a grip on her hand, his own hand fall away as the room became dark.

I love you, Emma.

He wished his mouth would voice the words.

★ ★ ★

The naval sick bay ward was quiet. Emma sat next to the bed and watched Jorge sleep, listened to him breathe. She couldn't believe how long his lashes were. They almost rested on his cheekbones.

She stood and stretched, shaking her head to ward off such a strange thought She'd kept vigil beside him ever since they got back to the base last night.

As soon as the sand storm passed, helicopters came, and Jorge was the first loaded, Punjabi the second. With the two stretchers, there was room for one other person, and she knew Osbourne had to go. Norton put her on the next flight out, and the twenty-minute flight back to their base took forever. On the helicopter, she'd studied the blood on her hands. Jorge's blood.

He'd stepped in front of Punjabi and took the blow intended for her. A blow that never should have happened because going into a tactical debriefing with a weapon in her boot was a huge rookie mistake. She couldn't believe she'd been so stupid.

And distracted.

Her mind hadn't been on the mission most of the time. As a result, Jorge lay in a hospital bed, clinging to life.

She knew they planned to move him to Germany first thing tomorrow and had already been told she couldn't go with him.

When she turned back around, she jumped, startled to see his eyes open. Then she rushed forward and took his hand. "Hey," she said quietly.

His grip was weak. He stared at her, the gold flecks in his eyes shining in the dim light. "I lived," he said in a hoarse voice.

Tears immediately came to her eyes. "Barely. Osbourne said another minute and it would have been a little harry. He held the knife perfectly steady for the ride back to base, stayed in the operating room holding it until the surgeons could do their thing."

He closed his eyes. She had so much she wanted to say to him, but he didn't need her emotional dump right now. While it might make her feel better it certainly would do nothing for him. It could wait.

Finally, he looked at her again. "Emma," he whispered.

She leaned over the bed. "Shh. Ozzy said the knife didn't hit your heart. It was a little too close for comfort, though."

His face had lost so much color. The pinching around his mouth and eyebrows told her he was in a lot of pain. "I'm glad you're here," he said.

"I'm sorry, Jorge." More tears filled her eyes. How many times was she going to cry today? "I'm so sorry."

"Why sorry?" He closed his eyes and winced.

"I never should have had my knife on me. I wasn't thinking. Then, seeing it sticking out of you...." Her breath hitched.

The nurse came around the partition and said, "You're going to need to go now. Doctor's coming."

She wanted to fight and kick and scream. Instead, she

stood and leaned over, pressing her lips to Jorge's forehead. His skin was hot and dry. "I'll see you later," she promised. He didn't open his eyes.

Determined not to walk down the streets of the base crying, she stopped in the women's restroom and washed her face. She met her eyes in the mirror. "He'll live. He's going to be okay. Get ahold of yourself."

Inhaling deeply through her nose and slowly releasing it from her mouth, she squared her shoulders and then left the restroom. The bright sun outside surprised her. Osbourne had wheeled Jorge into surgery the night before. Somehow, she still expected it to be dark outside.

When she got to her building, she put her hand on the handle as she heard her name. "Selah!"

When she turned, she spied Fisher jogging toward her. "Daddy wants you. Urgent." When she started to pivot, he added, "He said be ready to talk to Punjabi."

"Roger." She hadn't expected Punjabi to be ready for an interview for another few days. Jorge had fired three shots as he went down. Two hit Punjabi. One in the shoulder, another grazed his temple. Last she heard, he hadn't regained consciousness yet.

She threw open her door and rushed to the pack she had tossed onto her cot. She dug through it and pulled out her tablet. She started to look for her scarf but remembered using it to stem the flow of Jorge's blood. Her hands faltered at the mental image, but then she reminded herself that he'd live.

She grabbed another scarf from her locker and followed

Fisher to the medical building. As she jogged along the streets of the base, she tried to shed the emotions about Jorge and refocus on the mission. Punjabi was planning something. She knew it was imperative that she find out what.

CHAPTER
★
THIRTEEN

The sun was just breaking through the night sky bringing purple and orange dawn when Jorge walked out of the gym. He crossed the parking lot, tossed his bag into the back of the Jeep, then leaned against the door and looked up at God's early morning canvas. Physically, he felt better, normal. With an absent motion, he rubbed at the scar on his chest. He'd gone to Germany to convalesce. As soon as the doctors cleared him to return to the States, he headed back to his barracks room in Fort Bragg.

His team would arrive tomorrow. That would let him get back to work. There was always another mission to go on, another bad guy to track down and capture.

Spiritually, emotionally, he felt exhausted. Waking up in that clinic bed and finding Emma there had sparked a hope in him that gradually extinguished over the last five weeks. He expected her to write or call. Instead, he got radio silence. Maybe when the emotions of the day cleared, she realized that she couldn't actually let things go after all.

He sighed and got into the Jeep. His muscles burned from the workout he'd gotten teaching the black belt Taekwondo class. In the back of his mind, his inner voice called him a wimp for driving the less than two miles back to his barracks, but he reminded that voice of the knife that had come shockingly close to his heart muscle just six weeks ago and shut it up. He could jog it another day.

When he pulled into the parking space, he shut off the Jeep and just sat there for a moment. Everything would get better when the team came back. He believed it. He would feel less alone.

Finally, he opened the Jeep door and almost hit Emma with the door. She jumped back, gasping, then started laughing. He shook his head as if expecting her to disappear with the movement.

"Emma?" She didn't vanish. Still right there.

She put her hand over her chest and gasped. "Surprise," she said. "I honestly thought you'd seen me."

Without thinking, he got out of the Jeep and pulled her into his arms. She willingly went, and for a moment, he just relished the feel of her against him, the smell of her hair. He let her go and stepped back just enough to put his hands on her shoulders. "What are you doing here?"

"I came straight here. As soon as we finished the mission, I caught a hop."

He frowned and shook his head. "Mission?"

With raised eyebrows she asked, "You didn't know? Punjabi broke. We were able to capture the team he'd sent to bomb the U.S. Embassy in Cairo with a nasty chemical weapon."

He'd been so out of the loop. As the intelligence officer on his team, he knew everything about every mission. Even though he'd had to leave, the mission couldn't stop. Of course, that would completely explain the lack of communication from Emma. "You came straight here?"

Her smile lit her eyes. "I've been trying to get here for weeks."

He cupped her cheek with his hand, feeling the smooth skin. "Emma. You're really here."

She reached up and put both hands on the sides of his face. Her hands were cool. He closed his eyes at her touch. "Jorge, I want to spend hours talking with you, never stopping. But I promise that if you don't kiss me right now...."

He didn't need another word. Before she finished her sentence, his lips covered hers. Suddenly, everything in his world righted into place. She fit against him as if God designed her specifically for him. She smelled like strawberries and tasted like peppermint, a heady combination that made his head spin.

He wanted to pour himself into her, convey every thought, every feeling he'd ever had about her in just this conduit between their lips, but he pulled back. Gentling the kiss, intentionally slowing down to just savor the experience.

Soon, he lifted his head, brushed the hair off her forehead, and then pressed his lips against her skin. She leaned into him. In a husky voice she said, "That's better."

He grinned against her skin, then stepped back. "I couldn't understand why you weren't communicating with me."

"I know. I should have tried before I left, but I was just hours away. I thought I'd surprise you."

He snorted. "Color me surprised."

She looked around and then back at him. "Want to get breakfast? I haven't eaten since your yesterday."

He held out his hand. "I'll buy you breakfast at the chow hall."

"Sounds perfect."

She gripped his hand with both of hers and leaned against his arm as they walked. "How are you feeling?"

"Normal. It didn't hurt that much after Germany. Occasionally, I get a twinge of discomfort, but it's nothing like it was." They approached the brick building. Jorge opened the door. The fan above the door kicked on to keep insects from flying in. They ducked under the burst of air and then separated as they entered the chow line.

Jorge appreciated her appetite as she loaded her tray

with pancakes and scrambled eggs. He stuck with oatmeal. She piled cantaloupe and red grapes into a bowl at the fruit bar. He got them both coffee while she filled a glass with juice, then followed him to a small table near a window.

They bowed their heads. The touch of her hand on his surprised him. He turned his hand until their palms met and said aloud, "Father, thank You for safe travels for Emma, my healing, and this food. Bless it to the nourishment of our bodies and bless our bodies for Your service."

Emma echoed his, "Amen," then picked up her fork and knife and dug into the stack of pancakes. Around a mouthful of syrupy bread, she said, "I have been doing a lot of soul searching the last few weeks. I wanted to know what it was that made me so upset when I found out about your wife. In the end, it was two things."

His heart twisted in his chest. If he could go back and add one sentence to one conversation, this would never have happened. "What two things?"

"Your lie. In hindsight, I realize it wasn't malicious. You really didn't love anyone at home. But you were legally married, and that should have been part of some conversation at some point."

He nodded, not disagreeing. He swallowed a bite of oatmeal and asked, "And two?"

She sighed and set her fork down, picking up her cup of coffee. "And two, my own pride. Even though I know your situation, and you know your situation, no one else does. As far as anyone on that base at that moment knew, we were together, on the outskirts of a romance, and you were a married man. Do you know how many women fall prey to married men on deployment?"

"Emma —"

"It's okay, Jorge. I was embarrassed. Like, deep in my soul. But I'm okay." She set her cup down and leaned forward, her eyes shining with intensity. "When you got stabbed, all I could think was that I couldn't lose you. You couldn't die without knowing that I'd also fallen in love with you."

Emotion surged through his body, bringing the sharp sting of unexpected tears to his eyes. He could hardly believe her words. "I would go back and change the conversation if I could."

She smiled and held out her hand. He gladly took it. "I wish you could so that nothing could have come between us. I was distracted, and you got hurt. I'm sorry. I love you. I love you and everything about you. Almost losing you scared me."

He squeezed her hand, then let go. "So, where do we go from here?"

She dug back into her food. After she swallowed some eggs, she said, "I imagine that's a matter for discussion with God. I feel certain He has an idea."

Laughing, he shook his head and leaned back in his chair. "I'm looking forward to wherever He sends us."

"Me too."

Discussion Questions

Jorge answered Emma honestly about not loving anyone else and not having a girlfriend back at Fort Bragg. But he did not tell Emma about his marriage of convenience.

1. Do you think he lied by omission?

2. Do you think he was committing adultery with Emma?

3. Do you think Emma overreacted once she knew the truth?

Emma kills a man in combat and has an emotional reaction that she says she'll unpack later.

4. Do you think combat veterans emotionally suffer from the taking of human lives?

5. What can we as a society do to alleviate that suffering?

6. Do you think killing while in combat goes against the commandment "You shall not murder."?

When Emma is taken captive, she guesses the enemy plans to exchange her for Punjabi, a dangerous terrorist who planned to kill many people.

7. Do you think a trade is something her team should have considered if rescue wasn't an option?

8. Do you think this is a situation of "the good of the many outweighs the good of the few?" In other words, do you think Emma's life had a greater value than the people Punjabi targeted?

9. How should our perspective be different than those who do not follow Jehovah God?

Christ tells us to love our enemies and pray for those who persecute us (Matthew 5:44).

10. Do you think it's wrong to engage in warfare with our enemies?

Christ tells us that in this world we will have trouble, but to take heart because He has overcome the world (John 16:33).

11. Do you think that means we should ignore acts of terrorism and stay out of war?

12. Or do you think we are called upon to put on our armor and confront this "trouble" head on (Ephesians 6:13)?

Recipes

If you followed my Hallee the Homemaker website years ago, you know that one thing I am passionate about is selecting, cooking, and savoring good whole, real food. A special luncheon goes hand in hand with hospitality and ministry.

If you're planning a discussion group luncheon for this book, here are some suggestions to help your talk be a success. Quick as you like, you can whip up an unforgettable meal that is sure to please and certain to enhance the discussion and your special time of friendship and fellowship.

—— A Texas Tea ——

Emma and Jorge meet by providence in San Antonio when an unexpected storm drives them into a tea room. There they enjoy tea of course, and finger sandwiches, pastries, and Pico de Gallo to boot. Hey, it is San Antonio after all.

That afternoon, though they may not have realized it at the time, Emma and Jorge began to fall in love.

My prayer is that you will fall in love with this stormy afternoon tea the same way they did.

—— Hibiscus Tea ——

8 each	Hibiscus flowers
3 cups	water
1 TBS	fresh lime juice
	Honey to taste (raw honey is best)

This is a recipe for two cups. You need about 4 flowers per cup of tea.

Remove the calyx (the green part) from the flower which is attached to the plant. Remove the stamen (the part where the yellow seeds are attached.) Wash the petals under clean running water. Place in glass bowl or quart jar.

Bring water to a boil. Pour over the petals.
Cover and steep for 10-12 minutes.
Strain the tea.
Add lime juice.
Add honey to taste and serve.

— Cucumber Sandwiches —

1 large cucumber
8 oz cream cheese, softened to room temperature
¼ cup mayonnaise
¼ tsp garlic powder
¼ tsp onion salt
1 dash Worcestershire sauce
1 loaf bread, crusts removed
Lemon pepper

Thinly slice the cucumbers. Place between two paper towels and let drain for about 10 minutes.

Mix the cream cheese, mayonnaise, garlic power, onion salt, and Worcestershire sauce. Blend until smooth.

Spread cream cheese mixture evenly on one side of each bread slice.

Divide the cucumber slices over half of the bread slices.

Sprinkle lightly with lemon pepper.

Top with a bread slice.

Slice into triangles.

—— Cream Puffs ——

For the puff pastry

1 cup	water
½ cup	butter
1 cup	sifted unbleached all purpose flour
4	eggs

For the whipped cream

1 pint	heavy whipping cream
¼ cup	confectioners' sugar, sifted
1 tsp	vanilla extract

Preheat oven to 400° F (200° C)

In a medium saucepan, bring water and butter to boil. Reduce heat to low. Stir in flour. Stir constantly until mixture leaves the pan and forms into a ball (about 1 minute.)

Remove from heat and cool.

Beat in one egg at a time until well blended after each addition.

Drop by heaping spoonfuls onto parchment lined baking sheet. Bake 45-50 minutes, or until dry. Cool completely.

In a cool bowl, beat cream and sugar until peaks form. Beat in vanilla.

Using a pastry bag and tip, fill each puff pastry with sweetened whipped cream.

— Homemade Pico de Gallo —

4   large tomatoes
1   green pepper
1   red onion
2   jalapeño peppers (or other hot peppers)
1   bunch cilantro
    The juice from 1 lime

Remove the seeds and membranes from the peppers.

NOTE: When handling peppers, you might want to wear gloves so the capsaicin doesn't get on your skin and then, later, in your eyes. You'll thank me later.

Dice all the veggies into small cubes.
Separate the cilantro leaves from the stems. Discard the stems. Chop or tear the leaves.
Mix the veggies, cilantro, and lime juice together in a large bowl.
Serve with tortilla chips.

---- ★ ----

LOVED THIS BOOK?

Turn the page for a **SNEAK PEEK** at
the next in the series, *HONOR BOUND*.

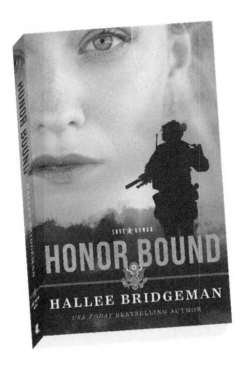

CHAPTER

ONE

KATANGELA, AFRICA

Captain Rick Norton crouched near the edge of the dirt road. Ears still ringing from the intense firefight, the smell of gunpowder burning his nose, he looked around, counting team members. Gerald "Jerry Maguire" McBride and Daniel "Pot Pie" Swanson came out of their hidden and elevated sniper-spotter positions. They both threw him a silent thumbs-up.

Travis "Trout" Fisher crouched nearby with his carbine pointed downrange and his radio rig tucked away. He also offered a thumbs-up. Jorge Peña "Colada" and Bill "Drumstick" Sanders glided backward toward his position with rifles at the ready. "Up!" they said in unison.

Rick scanned the jungle around him. "Ozzy, position?" No response.

His gut tightened, and he motioned for the men to regroup. Tension flowed through the team like electricity, then came a measure of relief when they found their combat medic, Phil "Doctor Oz" Osbourne, lying under a banana tree. He was trying to patch up his own thigh with a surgical clamp and a threaded needle below his hastily applied field tourniquet. Rick slid on his knees toward him and took the clamp from him.

"Caught one, Cap," Ozzy said, his voice hesitating as shock started to overtake his body. "No way I'm getting out of this jungle on my own two feet."

Wordlessly, Rick clamped Ozzy's artery despite its best efforts to worm up and out of sight, then wrapped a fresh field dressing bandage around his thigh, securing the clamp and protecting the wound.

"You don't know that, Doc," Sanders said. "I'd want Daddy patching me up if you were otherwise occupied."

Despite his tension, Rick internally rolled his eyes at the "Daddy" nickname. Sanders had drawled the words in an Alabama accent just to make them sound sweeter. Rick would address his mockery in a more appropriate manner, maybe with a bucket of ice water in some idyllic moment of downtime. For now, he let it slide and listened to Fisher calling headquarters for their extraction. He looked up expectantly as Fisher ended the radio call.

"They can pick us up twenty klicks from here, azimuth 26."

Twenty kilometers? With a quick calculation, Rick translated that distance to just over twelve miles. He scratched his red beard, estimated the amount of blood already lost, observed the rate it continued to soak into the field dressing, and concluded that Ozzy wouldn't make it two miles, much less twelve. He would lapse into hypovolemic shock before they could get halfway there, and he would undoubtedly expire soon after.

The team's military intelligence asset, First Lieutenant Peña, retrieved and studied the laminated map that hung from a snap ring on his pack. In his fascinating mind, Peña carried all their mission details. He had an olive-green bandanna tied close around his head but kept his curly black hair uncovered, and his heavy black beard was shaved close to his face. "There's a village two klicks east. Near the river. They have an American doctor, Cynthia Myers, in residence."

Rick pressed his lips together. He knew all about the American doctor. At least, he knew all about her father. "Any other options?"

"Drop packs," Peña said. "Four-man carry to the exfil LZ. Bounding overwatch. Rotate out every five to ten mikes."

Rick considered how long it would take for them to carry Ozzy through the jungle. Even after dropping their heavy packs and rotating in shifts, they would move too slowly. "It would take too long."

"Have them move up the exfil time or relocate the LZ. This is a PR, after all," Sanders said. Personnel recovery missions merited an elevated priority over routine combat operations and could require a more accessible landing zone.

"No-go on that one, Daddy," Fisher said. "Limited resources. Politically sensitive area and such. Azimuth 26 is the best we got."

Rick glanced at the blood-soaked bandage and nodded. Making his hand into a blade, he gestured toward the tree line. "Village it is. Maguire, Colada—fashion a stretcher. Trout, tell HQ to save their fuel for now. Pie, go collect some visibility on the AO until we're ready." He turned to Sanders. "You're on point with me, Drum. First leg."

"Check," Sanders said.

"Go get yourself a little recon while we partake of this incredible good fortune."

"Medals, Cap," Ozzy interjected, his tone dry. "Thanks of a grateful nation, for sure."

"You concentrate on stopping yourself from bleeding so much, Doc. I will take this time to plan our exfil, secure in the knowledge that this mission will doubtless earn us all legendary chest candy and fruit salad."

His team snickered. They did not do their jobs for

recognition. Green Berets had a reputation as the "quiet professionals" for a reason.

Using a nylon-poncho liner and some cut-down saplings, they fashioned a makeshift stretcher and carefully lifted Ozzy onto it. Sanders returned with a nod, indicating a clear path.

"Trout, toss your rig and Doc's pack on there too," Rick said. "You and Jerry Maguire make like Sherpas for Doc Oz. Pie, take overwatch for the first klick. Drumstick and I got point out of the gate." He focused on the tall Black man with the thick black beard and shaved head slicing an apple with his razor-sharp K-BAR knife. With the name Daniel Swanson, everyone called him Pot Pie. "Pie, when we arrive, stand to. You and Colada establish a home base close to the village. Bring silence to bear if the situation screams for it."

"Roger, wilco, Cap," Swanson said with a nod.

"Any questions or suggestions?" Rick searched his men's faces in the ensuing silence. "Right. Let us know if your little arms get tired, ladies. Let's roll."

Doctor Cynthia Myers had made her way to a remote village in Katangela to run an OB clinic and was the only doctor within several kilometers. Women came from villages all around for care. In the five months she'd been here, Cynthia had witnessed people dying of everything from infection to sickness to mortal wounds sustained in a hippopotamus attack.

As she stood in the dirt courtyard in front of the clinic, she watched a chicken with a fat grub clutched in its beak strut from the edge of the jungle. "You're going to get in trouble, Amelia," she said. The hen had become known as Amelia Egghart because she tended to explore the outside world as often as possible. "Tadeas doesn't like it when you escape from the coop."

Suddenly, ominous sounds interrupted her. From somewhere in the distance came the faint but unmistakable sound of automatic gunfire. Despite the isolation of the remote village in the wild of the African jungle, she had heard that sound all too often since her arrival.

The sounds escalated, a set of low, thunderous cracks alternating with short but sharp high-pitched bursts, like a distant percussion section warming up for a marching band concert at halftime. Something about these cracking reports sounded very different and threatening.

Her nurse, Tadeas, came out of the hospital building. "Apparently, there are more than just Kalashnikovs in the jungle today," he said.

"Pistols?" Cynthia asked.

He shook his head. "ARs. American rifles. Western mercenaries love expensive black rifles. The locals favor AKs. Those are cheap, and so are the bullets."

She felt her eyebrows knitting together as she listened to the now-sporadic gunfire. "That sounds close."

Tadeas turned his eyes toward the tree line. "Actually, that sounds very close."

Though they were nearly always fatal, the American-made 5.56 caliber rounds—much like the Kalashnikov 7.62 caliber rounds—created overwhelming trauma whenever patients survived the gunshots.

Meeting Tadeas's eyes, Cynthia saw her own worry reflected. "I'm going to go find something to eat," she said. "See if you can relieve Ayo. She may not want to leave Gamila yet, but she needs to eat something."

Gamila had gone into labor at four that morning. For six hours, Cynthia and Ayo, her midwife-in-training, had ministered to the teenager as she progressed through the labor. Having witnessed the growing infatuation blossoming between Tadeas and Ayo, Cynthia had no doubt that he would see to her trainee's needs now.

"One of the villagers brought your dinner, Doctor. I covered it and put it in your pantry," Tadeas replied.

He ducked into the doorway of the clinic, and she walked across the dirt courtyard into her own simple one-room home. She poured some water into the washbasin and wet a clean rag, then scrubbed her face, neck, and arms with the soap. As she rinsed with the cool water, inhaling the lavender scent, she felt ready for another five or six hours of work before she could safely call it a day.

Cynthia rebraided her hair, put a fresh bandanna around her neck, and unbuttoned her shirt, then slipped it off her shoulders. Wearing just her tank top and jeans, she sat on her cot and bowed her head. "God? Thank You for bringing me here, even amid the circumstances that perpetuated my decision. And thank You for the life You brought into the world today. Be with Gamila and give her wisdom in parenting."

As she lifted her head, her stomach gave an audible growl. Remembering Tadeas's words, she opened the cupboard above her sink and found some fried bread and a mango beneath a napkin of cheesecloth. She bit into the bread and closed her eyes, enjoying every flavor. Just as she put her knife to the skin of the mango, she heard the unmistakable sound of a truck engine revving high, followed by gunshots and a woman's fearful cry.

Stomach twisting, Cynthia jumped to her feet, slipped the knife into her pocket, and threw her shirt back over her shoulders. Stepping out into the courtyard just as a truck came to an abrupt halt directly in front of the clinic, she shielded her eyes and nose. Dust thrown up by the truck tires swirled around the vehicle, momentarily obscuring it in a powdery reddish-brown cloud.

As the dust settled, a man yelled out, "Where is the doctor?" He stood in the bed of the truck, wearing an unbuttoned olive-green uniform shirt with brass ammunition belts crisscrossed over his chest like bandoliers. In his hand he clutched a nasty-looking rifle with a drum-sized ammunition magazine. Out of the corner of her eye, Cynthia saw villagers ducking into the nearest buildings.

Angry at the violence that had once again permeated her peaceful home, she pushed back any fear she might have felt, stepped forward, and lifted her chin. "Hey, you! I'm the doctor."

Using the side of the truck as a brace, he vaulted to the ground and approached her, looking her over from the top of her braided hair to the toes of her size 4 brown leather boots. "You? You are the doctor?" he asked with a snarl.

"Yes. I am." Despite the fear that made her stomach clench, she held his gaze and waited.

Finally, he stepped back and gestured toward the truck as the driver got out and walked to the back. He opened the tailgate, reached in, and pulled something forward. "Save this man's life."

"Tadeas!" she yelled, walking toward the back of the truck. "I need gloves!"

As her nurse emerged from the clinic, the two men leveled their weapons in his direction. Rounding on the apparent leader, Cynthia said, "You want my help? I need my nurse."

Speaking in French, he granted Tadeas passage. Tadeas handed her two pairs of gloves and her stethoscope. His eyes screamed at her to use caution with these men. She didn't know how to reassure him or if she even should, so she thanked him.

Without warning, the driver kicked Tadeas in the back of his knees, bringing him to the ground. Before she could even gasp, he put the muzzle of his rifle against the back of Tadeas's head. Knowing that the man would not hesitate to kill him, she decided not to react as she slipped one pair of gloves into her pocket and put the other pair on.

When she approached the rear of the truck, she saw a young man lying atop a pallet on the open tailgate. Spent shell casings littered the truck bed. The smell of gunpowder mixed with blood filled her mouth with a metallic taste and almost overwhelmed her. Inspecting the patient, she saw his olive-green shirt soaked with blood. When she pulled the knife out of her pocket, the warlord put a hand on her wrist.

Cynthia looked into his wild brown eyes. "You can hinder me or stay out of my way. The choice is yours."

"Be very careful, Doctor. I have the power to kill everyone here. Their lives are in your hands." He released her.

She stripped the gloves off and dropped them to the dirt. She retrieved the second pair and carefully put them on. "Please don't touch me again. I have no intention of hurting your man here. But by interfering, you have just delayed my examination and put his life in further danger."

The man snorted but took a step back. She turned to the patient and ignored the fact that the man watched with bald suspicion as she cut the bloody shirt away. When she set the knife down, he picked it up and closed the blade, setting it far enough away that she couldn't easily grab it, and of course contaminating it. Cynthia shook her head in frustration at the man's stubborn stupidity.

Trying to put him out of her mind, she examined her patient. Two bullets had penetrated his right lower abdomen. She suspected the rounds were 5.56 caliber based on the size of the entry wounds and the trauma. Even in a stocked hospital with trained emergency staff, she couldn't see saving this man. He bore a brand on his inner wrist—the bull's-eye mark of Chukuwereije, a warlord who had grown in strength over the last five years. If she did not give the appearance of trying to save him, Tadeas would die. And likely Ayo. Maybe even her.

Heart pounding, she put her stethoscope to his chest. Shallow breaths, thready heartbeat. Moving the stethoscope down, she listened. No bowel sounds. He was so close to death. Without God's hand, nothing would change the inevitable.

Even as that thought crossed her mind, he took his last rattling breath. Had they noticed? Pushing her fingers against his neck, she searched for a pulse but found nothing.

Could she pretend he was still alive for a few minutes, stall them until she figured out a way to get Tadeas out of this mess? Probably not. These men had likely seen more death in their young lives than she would in her entire life. She had no options. Just as she took her stethoscope out of her ears and prepared to tell these warlords that their friend had died, she heard a commotion.

From out of the woods on the edge of the village, two soldiers emerged wearing camouflaged uniforms. They held their weapons at the ready and walked in a surprisingly fast crouch, though their upper bodies remained perfectly stable and the muzzles of their rifles perfectly vertical. They moved with practiced skill, looking like little tanks rolling across a smooth countryside.

The Chukuwereije soldiers started screaming orders.

The driver lifted his weapon and fired twice. One of the oncoming soldiers fired a single shot, and the man fell at Cynthia's feet. Before she could react, the leader grabbed her and put a pistol to her temple. The hot gunmetal pressed painfully against her skin.

Out of the corner of her eye, she saw Tadeas dash into the clinic. He likely went in to protect Ayo and Gamila. Once he was out of the way of any danger, she felt a sense of calm replace her rising panic.

Personal Note

I am so happy you read this prequel book that introduces the Love and Honor series. As the daughter of a U.S. Army Ranger, and the wife of a U.S. Army Special Forces soldier, this series came from deep inside my heart. I wanted to let my readers experience what it means to live and work as such an elite soldier, and I wanted a chance to celebrate the men and women who serve in our armed forces.

I pray that this book was a blessing to you. If it was, tell your friends about it. My favorite books throughout my life were all introduced to me by a friend.

Your word of mouth is the best way to spread the news

about this series.

Writing is often a solitary profession, but it doesn't have to be. I personally read every single book review, positive or otherwise. I'm not exaggerating.

It would mean the world to me if you shared your thoughts with me. Hearing from my readers helps me prayerfully craft the next story. An honest review also helps other readers make informed decisions when they seek an exciting, clean, romantic, suspenseful Christian book for themselves. Click any one of these links and leave your review. That is the next best thing to telling a friend and I promise to personally read it.

Goodreads:

www.halleebridgeman.com/lhp_gr

Bookbub:

www.halleebridgeman.com/lhp_bb

Amazon:

www.halleebridgeman.com/lhp_ar

I would LOVE IT if you would purchase *Honor Bound*, the next book in the Love and Honor series.

Honor Bound:

www.halleebridgeman.com/books/honor-bound/

Hallee Bridgeman is the *USA Today* bestselling author of several action-packed romantic suspense books and series. An Army brat turned Floridian, Hallee and her husband finally settled in central Kentucky, where they have raised their three children. When she's not writing, Hallee pursues her passion for cooking, coffee, campy action movies, and regular date nights with her husband. An accomplished speaker and active member of several writing organizations, Hallee can be found online at www.halleebridgeman.com.

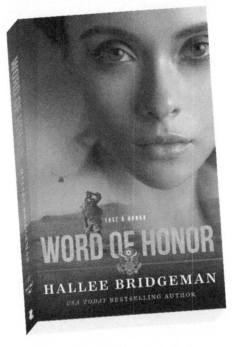

DEFEND FREEDOM
AND FIND LOVE WITH THE A-TEAM
IN HONOR'S REFUGE

AVAILABLE NOVEMBER 2022

Phil Osbourne of the Special Forces A-Team returned home from the military missing a leg and feeling like half a man, but Melissa Braxton has loved him almost since they met. When things take a dangerous turn at the domestic abuse shelter where Melissa works, Phil must overcome wounds both seen and unseen to find a strength long buried—and save the woman he loves.

MEET
HALLEE BRIDGEMAN

HALLEEBRIDGEMAN.COM

authorhalleebridgeman

halleeb

halleebridgeman

MORE BOOKS BY HALLEE BRIDGEMAN

Find the latest information and connect with Hallee
on her website: www.halleebridgeman.com

FICTION BOOKS BY HALLEE

The Song of Suspense Series:
A Melody for James
An Aria for Nick
A Carol for Kent
A Harmony for Steve

The Jewel Series:
Sapphire Ice
Greater Than Rubies
Emerald Fire
Topaz Heat
Christmas Diamond
Christmas Star Sapphire
Jade's Match
Chasing Pearl

PARODY COOKBOOKS BY HALLEE

Newsletter

Sign up for Hallee's monthly newsletter! Every newsletter recipient is automatically entered into a monthly giveaway! The real prize is never missing updates about upcoming releases, book signings, appearances, or other events.

Hallee's Newsletter: Hallee's Happenings

www.halleebridgeman.com/newsletter/

Made in the USA
Coppell, TX
15 January 2023

11144332R00111